A
MOON BOY
Loves
my BEST FRIEND

WRITTEN and ILLUSTRATED by
REBECCA PATTERSON

ANDERSEN PRESS

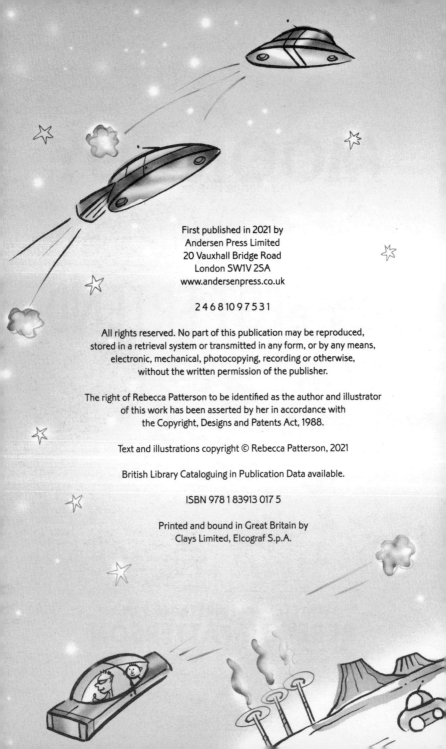

First published in 2021 by
Andersen Press Limited
20 Vauxhall Bridge Road
London SW1V 2SA
www.andersenpress.co.uk

2 4 6 8 10 9 7 5 3 1

British Library Cataloguing in Publication Data available.

ISBN 978 1 83913 017 5

Printed and bound in Great Britain by
Clays Limited, Elcograf S.p.A.

For Marina Ristuccia

CHAPTER ONE

'No one,' I said to my best friend Bianca, 'wants to go to Flooded Plains Water Adventure Camp! No one!' We were on our way to school on our flykes, flying high above the trees and houses, just turning down towards the school playground. I braked a little as we began to fly down. 'Everyone said it was terrible last year – cold, boring and babyish! Plus it's only four minutes away by skybus, it's in Norfolk! How can they call it an adventure camp if it's in Norfolk?!'

Bianca shrugged, 'Kayaking? Eating s'mores? Building campfires?'

We landed our flykes and put them in the flyke shed.

I raised my eyebrows at Bianca, 'Kayaking? S'mores?

No thank you, Grandma! It's sooo old fashioned. Plus they don't let you build a real fire, you just sit around a hologram of one.'

We heard a faint hum above us and looked up. Far up in the sky, just below the clouds, Mercedes was showing off in her persojet. She's the only kid who has one in our school. She got it from her auntie in Florida last year. Mercedes drew a smiley face with the pink vapour trail, before flipping over in a loop the loop and zooming down. She landed next to us with a bit of a skid and shook her hair out of her helmet. 'Did you see that?! My persojet skills are on fire. I could be an intergalactic pilot, I'm that good!' Then she looked at me. 'Ooh, look at little old sulky face! What's wrong with you, Lyla?'

'She's complaining about the residential trip.' Bianca smiled. 'Lyla says you can't have adventures in Norfolk and the camp is only for old ladies who like eating s'mores!'

'Lyla's right!' said Mercedes. 'My mum went to Flooded Plains when she was a kid, it was clank then and it's clank now. They have these little dome tents that let in the rain. How primitive is that?!'

We began walking towards the classroom portal together as a three. Amia ran up behind us. 'Hi! What's all this?'

'We're talking about how no one wants to go to Flooded Plains Water Adventure Camp!' I said.

'Ugh! I know!' said Amia. 'It sounds gross. Billie Luna-Jones, who went last year, said they saw an actual real live RAT. As big as a cat, two feet from their sleeping dome! Even Mr Caldwell was scared.'

'No way!' said Mercedes, shoving her coat into the suction hatch in the coatpod.

'Yes way!' went on Amia, arranging her hair a bit. 'And the food is really bad, Billie Luna-Jones said she got food poisoning from a caterfilla salad, plus they just have really old robots like Mr Martinelli supervising all the activities, even on the mile-high zip line so it's actually seriously DANGEROUS!'

I stood still for a second. Then I said, 'So let's not go! I'll get a petition going to campaign for a better residential trip. I'll get everyone to sign and tell Mr Caldwell we demand a better trip!'

Amia and Mercedes looked doubtful. 'Dunno if that will work,' said Mercedes, and walked into the class hub.

Amia shrugged her shoulders at me. 'We probably don't have time now, Lyla.'

I watched her saunter into the class hub too.

'I bet if Mercedes suggested it, everyone would sign a petition. That lot never listen to me.' I shoved my coat into the suction hatch.

'Well, maybe Flooded Plains Camp place will be OK,' said Bianca.

'Rats the size of cats!' I said, mostly to myself, as I walked into class. 'No thanks! I'm starting a petition! I'm starting it today. First break.'

And that's what I did. Bianca signed it first and then she came with me as I took it round to more people.

A MOON BOY LOVES MY FRIEND

'Didn't know you could be so ... persuasive!' laughed Bianca, as I stopped a whole basketball game to get Burak and James to sign.

Mercedes saw me get Ibrahim, and all the boys who sit in the corner at break swapping little football clones, to sign it. 'Wow!' she said. 'Didn't think you'd get that lot to sign, they don't care about anything except footie!'

'They care about rats the size of cats.' I smiled.

Due to my suddenly 'persuasive' personality it only took two breaks to get everyone to sign my petition. Louis MacAvoy signed twice!

Bianca and I took it to Mr Caldwell at the end of the second break. He leaned back in his chair, 'Very enterprising of you, Lyla. Good leadership skills.' But then he said while he appreciated everyone had signed my petition, Flooded Plains Water Adventure Camp was much cheaper than many other residential trips and if we wanted to go anywhere else we'd all have to raise some extra money.

So because of my petition we had to have a bake sale every Thursday. And that meant Bianca and I had to spend every Wednesday making a tonne of cakes to sell. We normally did it at my house because we have a bigger kitchen and a new high-spec cookbot. Plus Bianca's mum is mess-phobic. We usually made about thirty blueberry bouncing buns because they were really popular. They always sold out first. They came out of the cookbot all lovely, little and round.

Once they're cooked, you
can pick them up and drop
them down onto your plate
and they bounce back up
so you can catch them in
your mouth.

One day, we forgot to add the bounce dust so they
didn't . . . bounce. Gus, my six-year-old brother, started
throwing them really hard on the surfaces, trying to make
them bounce back but just splatting them everywhere.
'They seriously don't bounce, Lyla!' he yelled. 'They just
SPLAT! They all SPLAT! SPLATTY SPLAT!'

Dad said that I was partly responsible for the mess, so I had to get out the vacuum bot and help Gus clear it all up.

Gus said he didn't need to use the vacuum bot. 'Why would I need that? I am Vacuum Boy! My superpower is suction!' And started to suck up the blueberry bun splats off the table with his own mouth!

Anyway, as we didn't have any blueberry bouncing buns for the bake sale that week Bianca said, 'We'll just have to throw money at the problem and buy some cakes to sell.' So we did. We got a bargain pack of Ring-A-Ding-Sing Doughnuts on the way to school because who doesn't love one of those? When they come out of the wrapper, they sing you a little song through the hole in the middle. It's not *great* singing, but it's funny. We sold them for double what we paid for them. Bianca said I was turning into some kind of business whizzkid.

A MOON BOY LOVES MY FRIEND

We had our bake sales outside our class hub just after school. Mr Caldwell let us take some tables out from the class hub. Mercedes was in charge of the stall because she's bossy and good at saying stuff to little kids like, 'You touch it! You buy it!' I did the money with Bianca, and Louis MacAvoy and James Defries did what they called 'Promotion and Advertising Strategy', which was just them running round the playground past all the parents and kids yelling, 'CAKES! WHO WANTS CAKES?' And, 'SAVE US FROM FLOODED PLAINS BORING CAMP!'

One Saturday Bianca's granny, who lives in the super-swanky Havendome, said we could come round to her beautiful pink house and cook a load of vintage-style cakes and sell them to her neighbours. 'They'll love it!' she said. 'Buying cakes just like our grandmothers might have eaten as girls!' So Bianca and I went.

'I cannot believe they ate cakes with these horrible little black things in!' laughed Bianca, as she looked at the old-fashioned cake mix. 'What are they, dried beetles?'

'They're raisins, dear!' said her granny. 'Rather rare now. Dried grapes. I've had some of them in the back of my cupboard for years!'

'Try one!' I dared Bianca.

She put one of the wrinkled little things up to her mouth. 'Ugh! I can't. How could people eat cakes with these in?!'

'Oh, they loved them back then!' smiled her granny.

'What are these things I'm trying to make?' I asked, getting the messy brown mix all over the place.

'That's going to be cornflake cakes!'

'Looks bad!' said Bianca. 'These cakes are so dull, brown and yucky! Are you sure this is what they ate?'

'I'm sure,' said Bianca's granny.

'Why can't we just use the cookbot to make them?' asked Bianca. 'That's what we do at Lyla's house. This is *so slow.*'

'Well, this is the ancient art of "Home Baking". Now you can see how hard our ancestors had to work to get their bake sales together!'

'Can we make them look better with some Lightie Uppy Frootz sprinkled on top?' asked Bianca.

'No, dear. Let's keep them authentic!' said her granny.

As we placed the cakes outside on one of her granny's little old-style tables, Bianca made a face at me and said under her breath, 'Who's going to buy lumpy brown cakes full of dead grapes?'

Turns out, only every old person living in the Havendome!

We had a queue!

And all of them paid double what we asked. Two very swanky old women approached our stall. One had that diamond glitter hair and the other had a genuine pink micro tiger in her fancy laser-trim basket. They had a massive squabble over who should buy the last authentic vintage cornflake cake. And the one with the diamond hair said, 'But I haven't *seen* a genuine cornflake since 2067!'

In the end we had to cut it in half.

'Wow,' said Bianca, adding up how much we'd made, 'they really love old brown cakes!'

It was all worth it! The week just before half term, Mr Caldwell said, 'Well, Year Six, I've got some very exciting news! Thanks to your extensive fundraising, this year's residential trip will not be at Flooded Plains Water Adventure Camp. You've raised enough money to get us somewhere *really* exciting. This year we are all going to . . . Camp Crater! On the . . . MOON!'

The class went crazy.

Totally crazy!

Franka burst into tears and hung off Felicity's neck going, 'Oh my total gosh! I am going to die right now this minute with happiness!'

Burak got out of his seat and started punching the air and spinning round going, 'Oh yeah! Oh yeah!'

And Mercedes was clutching her chest with her eyes shut, saying, 'I'm gonna faint!'

Louis threw a little learning cube at my head and when I turned round he was doing a thumbs up at me.

'OK, settle down, class! Settle down. Back in your seat, please Burak!' said Mr Caldwell. 'Yes, it's fantastic news. We're all off to Camp Crater just on the outskirts of the great Moon city of Catena Yuri, or the "Big Sparkle" as the Moonites call it. I haven't been up there for years. Absolutely brilliant! Now, you will need slightly different kit for this trip but luckily there are some old moonsuits and gravity boots in the PE store so no one will have to buy any new stuff. We'll try them on next Monday after registration.'

'Mr C!' said Amia. 'Can we pack little helper bots? Like the ones that dry our hair?'

'Yes, if you have room.'

'What about if we have pet cyborgs at home?' asked Louis. 'Can we bring them?'

'No,' said Mr Caldwell. 'It says in the brochure, "For health and safety reasons no electronic companions e.g. cyborg pets or robotic children, are allowed to attend Camp Crater."'

· ✳·⭐·✳ *

Everyone was chatting like mad in the coatpod at the end of school. When Bianca was putting on her coat, she smiled at me. 'Just think, if it wasn't for you and your petition, we'd all be going to eat s'mores in Norfolk with giant rats!'

'I know!' I said, all excited.

Louis got up and stood on one of the benches. He cupped his hands around his mouth and shouted, 'GUYS! GUYS! WE NEED TO SAY THREE CHEERS FOR LYLA!'

'Yeah, wait . . .' said Mercedes getting up on the bench next to Louis. 'Guys! I present Lyla Hastings! Class hero! She saved 6C from Flooded Drains Rat Camp!' And she hauled me up next to her and started shouting, 'SPEECH!'

So I did a little bow and said,
'I'd like to thank my assistants
Bianca, Mercedes, Amia,
Louis and James . . . and to
everyone who baked us into
this historic moment!'
I did a little fake sob
like they do at awards
ceremonies and then I
shouted, 'WE'RE GOING
TO MOON CAMP!' And
I punched the air.

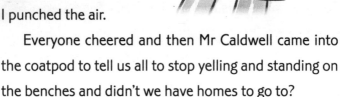

Everyone cheered and then Mr Caldwell came into the coatpod to tell us all to stop yelling and standing on the benches and didn't we have homes to go to?

As we walked across the playground Louis said, 'I'm in a daze. I'm actually going to the Moon Colonies. Me! I've only ever been as far as Hunstanton! Did you know kids are allowed to drive skycars up there? Not just stupid pedal flykes like us! I think all of them get a kid-size skycar when they're like three years old or something.'

'Yeah, right!' said Mercedes. 'I don't think so. Anyway, I really hope we get to go to the malls in Catena Yuri! They have *real* shopping up there. Not the stupid old Trading Hub with virtual everything and glitchy old robots trying to make cappuccinos.'

'Yeah!' said Amia. 'My mum's cousin had her wedding in Catena Yuri! She said it's amazing. They've created the "Optimum Living Experience" up there. Real actual malls with all the things you can actually touch and buy! And there's all these amazing parks! And everyone is beautiful! She went to the Luna Spa Thermal Pools and got her nails done with a real sapphire finish!'

'Pah! I'm not going to the Moon to get my nails done!' said Louis. 'I'm going for the crater climbing! They have craters miles high up there. And for the laser blaster archery! Boom!' And he ran to his flyke and started pedaling up into the air. 'SEE YOU MONDAY, MY FELLOW MOONITES!' he yelled as he flyked up high above us and off home.

Mum collected me and Gus that afternoon in our old skycar. Gus was already in his seat when I got in. 'You were ages!' he said.

'I was busy. Everyone had to clap me because I am the class all-time hero!'

'You?' said Gus, looking at me sideways, doubtfully. 'How?'

'Because I started the petition which started the bake sales which raised the money so our class residential trip is . . . ON THE MOON! It's basically MY trip to the Moon. I made it happen!'

'Oh well done, love! Nice to see you taking the initiative!' said Mum as she launched our car up into the Fly Zone with all the other flying cars.

'We're going to Camp Crater just outside Catena Yuri. We get to try on moonsuits and gravity boots on Monday!'

Gus folded his arms across his chest crossly. 'Not fair! I want to go to the Moon. I've only been to Florida. And Granny J's in Bootle!'

'You might go there when you're in Year Six, like Lyla,' said Mum as she powered our skycar up over a skylorry.

I looked out across the city with its buildings, bridges, launch pads and balconies, the view I'd seen all my life. There was the big, old Trading Hub, the Havendome where Bianca's granny lives, the same old houses, blue sky, clouds . . . I said softly to my reflection in the window, 'I'm actually going to . . . the . . . Moon Colonies. For real! In four weeks!'

'Yeah, well, Lyla Pyla-poo,' shrugged Gus, 'when I'm in Year Six I'm gonna have the biggest bake sale in the universe and my class will have our residential trip on MARS!'

CHAPTER TWO

Mr Caldwell got me and Louis to help him collect all the old moonsuits and gravity boots from the PE store the following Monday. They were all in big bags behind the gym mats, ping-pong bats and low-gravity tool sets. Mr Caldwell pulled the bags out. 'Phew! Don't think these have been used for a while! I think the last school trip to the Moon Colonies was back in 2088, when the football team went up there to play against another school. You grab this bag, Louis ... Lyla, can you carry that one? I'll take the biggest.'

We dragged the bags back to our class hub where Mr Martinelli had been left in charge of our class. He is such an old robot now. He's a sort of a caretaker bot, but he's really just a big old can with a few lights. He supervises classes by rolling to the front of the room and moving his little spindly wire arms about, going, 'QUIET. QUIET. QUIET.' But he has really basic sight sensors and he can't move his head much. So when Mr Martinelli is left in charge, Mercedes and Burak always see how far they can creep to the front of the room without him seeing. Which is what they were doing when Mr Caldwell and us two came back in with the moonsuit bags.

Mr Caldwell made them apologise to Mr Martinelli but Burak muttered, 'Why? It's like saying sorry to a dumb calculator!' So he had to miss break.

We all got the moonsuits and gravity boots out of the bags and started to try stuff on.

'THESE STINK!' shouted Amia.

'Yeah,' said James Defries, 'of mould!'

'OK, I'm not putting mine on!' said Felicity. 'I have allergies!'

'Well, I'm not putting mine on cos I look bad in bright orange!' said Mercedes.

'Don't be so silly!' said Mr Caldwell, already in his adult moonsuit and clomping around at the front of the class. 'They may not be brand new, but they work. We'll only have to wear them if we go outside the Camp Crater dome. Come on, let's get them on and have a trial walk round the playground.'

We put them on with the helmets. Most of the helmets were silver with clear visors and had scratches and patches where the silver had worn away. But two were a bit newer and a cool purple colour and had tinted visors, so everyone was trying to get them.

A MOON BOY LOVES MY FRIEND

Felicity grabbed a purple helmet from Burak shouting, 'BURAK! I NEED ONE OF THE NEW ONES FOR MY ALLERGIES!' Mr Caldwell said all the helmets were exactly the same and as long as they protected us from radiation, who really cares what colour they are?

'*Me*,' said Mercedes, under her breath. 'Cannot believe I'm finally going to the swanky Moon Colonies and I'm being forced to go in this stinky old junk! What if I bump into a celebrity looking like this? Everyone cool lives on the Moon. I might walk into someone like Astrid Venus! My all-time hero! What's she gonna think if I'm looking clank in this junk?'

Mr Caldwell didn't hear. He carried on clomping about in his suit and said he'd be sending the complete kit list out by the end of the week and further details about the camp's activities. He told everyone to come back into the class hub and change out of the suits. Louis MacAvoy stayed out in the playground doing a silly slow-motion moonwalk, then he took off his helmet and pretended to die from suffocation. He rolled about on the ground clutching his throat, going, 'Aaaagh, I'm too young to die!'

He had to miss break with Burak. Mr Caldwell made them fold all the suits up and put them back in the PE store.

On Tuesday Mercedes started her own petition to demand more stylish moonsuits for our trip. She was showing everyone pictures of the latest moonsuits you can get up in Catena Yuri on her interface. Amia, Felicity and Franka were standing around her saying stuff like, 'Oh my total gosh, that is so gorgeous! Look at the sequined helmet! Do they do that one in the rose gold colour?' Bianca and I didn't sign Mercedes' petition. James Defries didn't sign either. He said he liked the orange suits as they had a 'traditional vibe, like an old school Moon pioneer.' When Mercedes went to show Mr Caldwell her petition he just folded his arms across his chest and said moonsuits were so expensive that if she wanted to get a set of new ones for the class, she'd be doing bake sales for the next fifty years. She stomped back to her place muttering, 'I do not wear orange. I will *not* wear orange. Orange is so not my colour!'

On Wednesday Mercedes was still going on and on about how orange was not her colour and how she couldn't face going to the glitzy Moon Colonies in a manky old moonsuit. Mr Caldwell told her to stop whispering about it to us in maths. But on Friday she arrived at school all excited and did four massive loop the loops above the playground in her persojet before she landed really fast, letting out a massive plume of lilac smoke on the launch pad. She shouted down to us all in the playground, 'GUESS WHO'S GONNA BE LOOKING SMOKIN' HOT AT MOON CAMP?!'

Then she stomped down the launch pad steps towards us, doing a little sassy model walk, snapping her fingers. 'I'M SHOPPING TILL I'M DROPPING TOMORROW!'

'Why?' asked Amia.

Mercedes ran across the playground and joined us sitting on the wall outside the class hub as we waited for Mr Caldwell to let us in. She patted her hair and said, 'I got some extra cash.'

'How?' asked Bianca.

'From my auntie in Florida. I told her about those disgusting old moonsuits and she agreed I obviously need something more fashionable!'

'Obviously,' muttered James Defries.

'Yeah, *obviously!*' said Mercedes, crossly, '*You* might not mind turning up in the Moon Colonies looking like a load of dusty old Earthling losers, but *I* wanna look cool. It's a once-in-a-lifetime experience! Moon Camp residential!'

For a bit no one spoke as we thought about us all shuffling about the Moon looking like dusty old Earthling losers. Then Mercedes said more quietly, 'Anyway, who wants to come to the Trading Hub with me tomorrow to go and look at the Stellar Marz Fashion stuff? They have a load of designer moonsuits, all the new styles. I could order direct, but I want to see how they look in the Style-Me Zone. And get your guys' opinions.'

'I'll come,' said Amia. 'I can get some Moon Dust repellent and some Moonglare moisturiser at the same time.'

Bianca and I said we'd go too.

A MOON BOY LOVES MY FRIEND

That Saturday morning we all met outside the Trading Hub at eleven. The Trading Hub was built ages ago so it's not that great. It's mostly where people pick up their orders or get stuff teleported in. And there are some really sad looking places where old people drink cappuccinos while they wait for their bulky orders from China to come through the big old teleporters.

Mercedes led the way through the Trading Hub. As she walked she looked around at the old teleporter hatches and flickering hologram adverts for aquagro cereals. 'This place is so over! I cannot wait to get to a real Moon Mall! Crystal walkways. Actual shops with stuff in! Beautiful cyborg assistants showing me the latest jewel nail finishes! Shopping on the Moon is "Everything new, sold with old-style elegance", like it says on the adverts.'

We passed a small rusting robot helper. It was beeping out a greeting and had a bent antenna.

It said, 'May I? Fruit and Veg? Help you?' over and over.

'Piece of junk!' Mercedes muttered, rolling her eyes. 'That is not good customer service. This place needs a revamp! On the Moon, everything works and everything's shiny. *Fact.*'

The Style-Me Zone is in the far corner of the Trading Hub by the old escalator things. You can't go on those because they're historic. They're in a massive clear case, like a museum exhibit. They've kept them from ages ago with a plaque saying they used to be in some ancient shop on this site during the Petrol Era. Sometimes they have them running and little kids press their noses against the case to watch the stairs sliding up and down.

Mercedes went to the screen and chose some moonsuits to try. Then she stood on the shiny footprints on the floor and the virtual outfit appeared so it looked like she was wearing it. 'How's this one?' she said, twirling about in the virtual suit.

'A bit babyish!' said Amia. 'The kitten ears on the helmet are cute but that fluffy little tail is too much!'

Mercedes pressed the screen to try another.

'Too navy blue!' laughed Bianca. 'Like my mum would wear!'

Mercedes pressed again. We all laughed.

'What? What's so funny!'

'It's showing you dressed in a sort of old-lady party dress! There's a big poofy-out skirt!'

'Stupid glitchy thing!' said Mercedes, slamming the touch screen.

We all laughed again. 'Now you look like Mrs Fradley in her headteacher suits!'

'You lot try! Make sure it's on "Moonsuits – Designer Brands"!' yelled Mercedes.

'We'll try!' I said. 'But the screen's so dirty, I don't think it's working properly.'

'This place is a total dump!' muttered Mercedes.

Then, for fun, Amia set it to 'Furniture – Seating' and the next thing, Mercedes looked like she was wearing a big, fat armchair.

'OK! That's not funny,' she said. 'Get me back into my moonsuit!'

Eventually Mercedes chose a very shiny pink and purple suit. It was much tighter fitting than the ones we have at school. She did her model walk in it in the Style-Me space and we all admired her. 'Looks AMAZING!' squealed Amia. 'Look at the logo – it goes all down the arm!'

'Yeah! I know! And check out the boots I'm getting! These ones have Lunatex grips on the soles. It won't be *me* falling over Moon rocks, like you lot in your old massive brick boots!' She danced about a bit. The boots had cute little wing decorations on the heels. 'And check out the helmet!' She had on a very sleek helmet with an iridescent visor. 'So much better than the buckets they have at school! I could actually see through this!' she said. 'OK! I'm ordering and getting it teleported to my house today!'

Bianca and I were shocked by how much it all cost. On the moving walkway to the Pharmacy Zone we said to Mercedes, 'You could have bought half a skycar or seventy-eight robocats for that!'

'Yeah, well I don't need seventy-eight robocats, do I?' said Mercedes, marching in front. 'But I do need to be Moon Colony-cool!'

In the Pharmacy Zone we tested all the Moon Dust repellents and Moonglare moisturisers. They had these helper bots who were so old and rusted-up they couldn't tell how much we were using. We put on loads of stuff for free. Mercedes didn't try them, as she said the helper bots looked dirty. While we were smearing all the different stuff all over our hands and sniffing them, Mercedes just leaned against a pillar and sighed, 'I do really want to go on the residential trip, you know I'm totally looking forward to it. But six days is a long time to be away.'

'It's nothing!' I said, patting a glob of Galactic Grape-scented gel onto my left hand.

'Well, it's not long for someone like you, but for me it's different,' sighed Mercedes, looking down at the floor.

'Er, why?' said, Bianca raising her eyebrows as she sniffed a tube of Mango Moon Protect Plus.

'Because I'm gonna be missing someone . . . special,' said Mercedes.

Amia stopped smearing stuff on her hand. 'Who? Your mum?'

'No, not my mum, silly!' said Mercedes, smirking and looking sideways and mysterious.

'So who?' asked Bianca.

We all stopped sniffing and smearing stuff and looked at Mercedes. She gave another little smirky smile and said quietly, 'My . . . *boyfriend.*'

'Since when have you had a boyfriend?' I said.

'Kind of since ages,' she shrugged. 'He's called Kelvin Cooley, and he's shorter than me but he's almost twelve.'

'Oh my gosh!' said Amia. 'Is he the one from next door to you?'

Mercedes nodded and said softly, 'We've known each other since we were babies and we just realised last week how much in love we are.'

'Have you kissed him?' said Amia, all excited.

'Maybe,' sighed Mercedes. 'Anyway, we need to get going, it's almost twelve and I've got Low Gravity Jazz Dance at one. Choose your stuff, Amia!'

Amia chose a Cherry Comet Moonglare moisturiser and some Moon Dust repellent in the same smell.

As we all went back to get our flykes, Amia kept asking Mercedes about Kelvin Cooley: about his hair, his house, his pets, his favourite ice cream.

Bianca whispered to me, 'How much more Kelvin Cooley can we take?'

And I whispered back, 'Well . . . we don't know his favourite colour or his middle name yet.'

Bianca bit her lip and tried not to laugh but Mercedes swung round and said, 'Yeah well, little girlies, I don't really expect *everyone* in Year Six to understand this stuff yet!'

As Bianca and I flyked above the trees back to our houses, Bianca said we shouldn't worry about it. Mercedes has been full of herself since she started Reception and she's OK really. Then we had a really fun time saying, 'I'm Kelvin Cooley and I love you truly!' in silly voices, right until I landed on my launch pad and waved as Bianca flew on home.

CHAPTER THREE

'MUM!' yelled Gus. 'LYLA'S MADE AN EARTHQUAKE IN HER ROOM! COME AND LOOK!'

'Ssh!' I said. 'She knows. I'm packing for my Moon Camp residential.'

Gus put on a silly high-pitched voice to mimic me: '*My Moon Camp residential.*' He wandered around my messy room. 'This isn't packing! This is exploding!'

I counted out socks onto the floor and smoothed my pyjamas into a neat folded square. Gus picked up my Moon Dust repellent and squirted some of it out of the tube. 'Not on my socks!' I shouted. 'Pass me that stuff and Nano Ted, he's coming with me. And my hair brush. Don't just throw them! Pass them!'

A MOON BOY LOVES MY FRIEND

Gus sat down on my little case. It has small jets on the bottom so it can hover behind you as you pull it along. He pressed the buttons to make the jets work and floated up off the ground.

'You'll never fit all that stuff into this!'

'I will. Get off the case. I need to start putting it all in.'

Gus turned off the jets and got off. I started trying to cram all my stuff in.

'You'll have to leave out your clean knickers!' said Gus. 'Smelly bum.'

'Not if I really press everything down!'

I got Gus to sit on the case lid so I could do it up. He looked at me from under his messy fringe and said, 'Will you miss me when you're on the Moon?'

'It's only a few days,' I said. 'And it's going to be the best time ever! So I don't think so.'

Gus tipped his head on one side, trying to do his cute face.

'Can I play in your room while you're away?'

'NO!' I said, pulling my case down the corridor to the front door so that it would be all ready for tomorrow. 'You can't go in my room. You can't even stand in the doorway and look at my room. And that's an order!'

'Smelly bum,' said Gus, picking up Sparks, our cyborg cat. 'Sparks thinks you're mean and he says he likes me best. He says he hopes you have a horrible Moon trip.'

'Sparks can't talk.'

'He can to me!' said Gus, putting our little robocat down and stomping into the kitchen.

· ✳ ⭐ ✳ ·

After tea Gus was yelling about how it wasn't fair he wasn't going to the Moon and got into massive trouble for mashing some peas into the carpet on purpose. Dad said he was a little minx. In the end he had to go and calm down in his room and then Dad told him he'd have a brilliant week at home with Mum and Dad and if he was really good they could go to the Low Gravity Soft Play Centre on Tuesday after school and it would be fun.

'Not the same fun as the Moon,' muttered Gus.

A MOON BOY LOVES MY FRIEND

But he did get up really early next morning to say goodbye. He hugged me and said, 'Lyla, I don't really hope you have a horrible trip to the Moon.'

'I know,' I said patting his head. 'And think! When you look up at the Moon at night you can wave and I might be waving back from my Camp Crater camp bed!'

'Come on,' said Mum. 'They want everyone at the school gates for seven-thirty. Let's get into the car, Lyla!'

I looked down at Gus waving from our front portal as Mum flew the car up into the Fly Zone. It was so early there wasn't much traffic flying about.

When we arrived everyone was in the playground with their floaty pull-along cases and snacks for the journey. James Defries was in his Moonshades. Mr Caldwell was ticking people off the register. I noticed at seven-thirty the cleaning bots were still sliding up the domed sides of the school, cleaning the windows. I said goodbye to Mum and then stood next to Bianca.

Felicity was crying and hugging her mum who was stroking her hair and saying, 'It's not that long, sweet pea, just five sleeps!'

Felicity was wiping her nose with her hand and saying, 'But it's not like just going to Granny's house, it's the actual Moon! I'm scared!' She had a new little travel bag in the shape of a flower over her shoulder.

Franka arrived and said 'Don't worry, Mrs Phillips, I'll look after Felicity! She can have one of my Space Pace calming tablets, they're lemon flavour. Want one, Flissy? Look, I've got a whole spare packet. You can have it!'

Felicity sucked on a Space Pace tablet and tucked the rest of the packet into her flower bag, watching her mum walk away. Her mum kept turning back and waving with both hands and blowing kisses to Felicity, right until she went out of the school gates.

When we heard the hum of the arriving skybus, everyone started cheering and looking up into the sky. And then we all clapped when it landed. It was a bit bigger than the skybus they use for normal school trips. It had those big Lunajets at the back. It said, *Sneddon's Skybuses – To the Moon and Beyond!* on the side.

The bus driver was old and jolly. He climbed down from the bus quite slowly and said, 'Right! Who's ready to go to the Moon!'

Mr Caldwell said we were just waiting for one more but we could start getting our cases into the hatches.

A MOON BOY LOVES MY FRIEND

Louis asked the driver where else the skybus went. 'It says, "To the Moon and Beyond" on the side, where's "Beyond"?'

'Oh . . . that's just advertising,' laughed the jolly driver. 'Moon's the limit with these jets! I don't think we'll be pushing onto Mars in this old thing!'

Mr Caldwell looked at the time and sighed. 'Where *is* Mercedes?'

Just then a very flashy new skycar landed in the playground just a few feet from where we were waiting. Mercedes almost fell out of the side door carrying several bags and snacks. She'd dyed her hair an amazing green colour since yesterday. Her mum got out the other side, bringing a few more bags and a massive silver pillow shaped like a crescent moon. Mr Caldwell reminded Mercedes' mum that you can't park in the playground and she should always land her skycar on the launch pad for health and safety reasons.

'What! Park right up there and then have to carry all her stuff down those steps? I don't think so!' said Mercedes' mum. 'Here you go, babe,' she said to Mercedes, handing her the massive moon pillow and the other bags. 'Be good!' She got back into the skycar and shouted out as she took off, 'Bring me a present, Mercie!'

'You're late,' said Mr Caldwell, as he started to count us onto the skybus.

'Sorry, Mr C, but I had loads to pack and then I got up really early to do my hair. We all wanna look good for Moon Camp!'

A MOON BOY LOVES MY FRIEND

'I suppose we do,' sighed Mr Caldwell, looking even more tired than he usually does and running his hand through his scruffy hair.

Bianca and I sat together in the middle of the bus, behind Mercedes and Amia and in front of James Defries and Louis MacAvoy. James and Louis were discussing different types of skybus.

Mercedes was discussing why she thought green was the most fashionable hair colour right now and how many times she'd had to message Kelvin Cooley this morning. 'He's SO sad!' she was saying to Amia. 'He doesn't know what he's going to do without me for so long!'

Bianca gave me a little look as we both listened. We heard Amia say it's only six days we're away but Mercedes said, 'Yeah, but when you're totally in love that's like for ever!'

Louis stood up in his seat behind us and shouted over our heads to Mercedes, 'You know Kelvin Cooley?'

'Why? What's it to you?' said Mercedes, turning round in her seat.

'Nothing. I just see him about. He's that little kid

with the scooter? Does his hair in spiky tufts?'

'He's not that little!' said Mercedes. 'He's eleven.'

'He's never!' said Louis. 'My mum knows his mum, he's nine. He's in Year Five at St Joseph's!'

Mr Caldwell told everyone to sit down and do their seatbelts up. And Mercedes stopped talking about her romance with Kelvin Cooley and started talking about her relaxing lavender moon pillow.

The bus driver fired up the jets and we were off!

'TO THE MOON AND BEYOND!' shouted Louis. Then he shouted, 'COME ON EVERYONE! THREE MORE CHEERS FOR LYLA'S MOON TRIP!'

Which was a bit cringey but quite nice. I smiled, bit my lip and looked down at the school and the playground disappearing into just a speck beneath the clouds. We were off to Moon Camp and it was all because of me!

CHAPTER FOUR

After about ten minutes into the trip Mr Caldwell stood up and floated in the low gravity down the aisle, pulling himself along the centre of the bus using our headrests. 'Now, I see a lot of you have started tucking into your snacks already. May I remind you that this trip to the West Moon takes at least two and a half hours, and that's if we don't get stuck in air traffic or the satellite beltway once we get closer to the Catena Yuri Zone.'

Louis finished his sandwich and packet of jellyfish crispies and wiped his mouth with his sleeve. 'Tasty!' he said. Then he shouted, 'Guys! We're going Moonwards! Let's get the energy up! Let's have a song!'

So everyone sang the old skybus classic 'We're a Mile in the Air But We Don't Care!'

Mr Caldwell normally stops us singing but he seemed so happy to be going on a really exciting trip that he joined in. Then he made us sing that old Moon Pioneer song called 'I Built My Shelter in the Dust'. Even the bus driver knew the words. I stopped singing after a bit and just looked out at the big blue Earth and all the shiny little specks of skybuses and short-range personal jets making their way to and from the Moon. I could see the outline of Britain poking out from under the swirly clouds and thought about Gus eating his morning fruit snack in his classroom down there.

A MOON BOY LOVES MY FRIEND

After a bit everyone calmed down and just looked out of the big windows. A few people played on their interfaces. Bianca was just wondering what the camp beds would be like – 'Maybe those really high triple bunk ones!' – when there was a sort of rumbling noise from the skybus engine. I saw the jolly driver (now looking less jolly) say something to Mr Caldwell.

'OK EVERYONE, LISTEN UP!' said Mr Caldwell. We all peered over the tops of the seats. 'Looks like we've got a bit of a problem with the rear Lunajet so Mr Cuddon, our driver, thinks we better call in at the next space service station to get it fixed.'

Everyone groaned.

The skybus slowed down and after a few minutes docked in the West Moonwayz Services. We weren't allowed to get off the skybus. I looked out of the window. I could see a little shop selling Moon souvenirs, quite cheap ones: inflatable moon rocks and teddy bears in moonsuits. A few tourists were bouncing about in their moonsuits and going to get drinks from the kiosk. I watched a little toddler in his tiny moonsuit bouncing about behind his mum. She'd put a line around his waist so she could keep him safe, and sometimes he floated up behind her like a balloon. There was a skybus parked right next to us full of old grannies drinking cups of tea. They had helmets on which said, *LUNA HIKING CLUB*.

After a bit the mechanic bots came and we all waited inside the skybus while they bashed about with the rear jet. Then a mechanic bot got onto the bus and explained in his robotty voice: 'Will have to or-der replace-ment sky-bus. This sky-bus not func-tion-ing.' This time even Mr Caldwell groaned.

A MOON BOY LOVES MY FRIEND

He said we could undo our seatbelts and could float about the skybus to stretch our legs. Actually, we didn't have to wait too long. Only ten minutes. Then an amazing new skybus parked right next to ours and we were transferred onto it through the airlocks while Mr Cuddon got out in his old brown bus driver's flightsuit and bobbed about transferring all our luggage. The new skybus had really good squishy seats.

Burak sunk into his squishy seat, stroking the armrests, going, 'Mmm, lovely, we've been upgraded.'

James was all excited, saying this skybus was made from Martian Titanium, 'Which is the absolute best!'

But when Felicity floated past me, still looking a bit cross and teary, she slowed down right by me, and hissed, 'This is all your fault, Sprouty Hair. Bake sales. Dangerous broken bus! If anything happens to me on this trip, it will be all because of *you*!' Then she floated off to her seat.

I had that sinking feeling in my tummy and bit my lip.

Bianca was sitting by the window now, looking out at the kiosk with the teddies in moonsuits. She turned to me and asked, 'What was Felicity saying to you?'

53

'Oh nothing, really,' I said. 'Just usual Felicity stuff.' I patted my hair. It is sprouty on one side normally but in this low gravity I could feel it was sprouty all over. I asked Bianca, 'Does my hair look really silly?'

'Everyone's does!' she laughed, swishing her own pink hair about. 'Low gravity equals zero style, you know that!'

The new skybus flew on up to the Moon. The Moon was now so close we could see all the cities on it. There was the great dome covering the whole of the city of Catena Yuri and thousands of rockets, skycars and skybuses zooming in and out of the city portals. The kids on the right side of the skybus like me and Bianca had the best view and everyone sitting on the other side got out of their seats and floated over to join us. Quite a few people floated in the aisle and some floated right over all of us.

Louis leaned over Mercedes to get a better look and yelled, 'There's the Catena Central Stadium! Where The Moon Ravens played West Mars F.C.!'

'MIND MY HAIR, you idiot!' said Mercedes.

'Look! And there's the Armstrong Tower!' shouted

Ridwan, bobbing about above me to get a better look.

Mr Cuddon spoke through his microphone, 'Children, I need you *all* to sit *back* in your seats with your seatbelts on. We cannot land safely with children floating all over the bus! Please sit DOWN!'

Then I heard Louis say to James, 'Hey! Wanna know how to swear in Moonite? You do this with your hands.' Louis was putting his two thumbs together and whispering the meaning into James' ear.

'That's bad!' laughed James. 'Who showed you that?'

'Saw it in a movie!' said Louis proudly.

'AND I HOPE WE WON'T BE SEEING THAT AGAIN!' shouted Mr Caldwell as he floated down the aisle checking everyone was back in their seats. 'That is unacceptable! Let me remind you that you are representing our school while we are at Camp Crater. Not only that, while we are up on the Moon you are all ambassadors for Planet Earth! I do not want to hear or see any bad language.'

Louis and James, embarrassed, looked down at their knees saying, 'Sorry, Mr Caldwell.'

Now we were so close to Catena we could actually see the weather inside the city dome, the clouds, the trees and the beautiful houses. 'I can see the mall!' shouted Mercedes. 'Stop here!'

But the skybus didn't enter the huge city dome, it flew on. Over the outskirts of Catena Yuri with its deserted little old villages from pioneer times (like we've drawn in history) and then on over the bare white Moon deserts.

'Where's this dump?!' shouted Mercedes. 'This is just a big, fat, dusty, dirty nowhere! Me and Amia want to get our nails done!'

'Camp Crater isn't in the middle of the city,' explained Mr Caldwell. 'It's just outside, near the great mountain ranges. Didn't you look at the information I sent out?'

'What the . . .' said Mercedes huffily, crossing her arms over her chest. 'If I'd known *that* I'd never have done all the bake sales! I thought the Moon was swanky! It *is* swanky in that show *Lucy Loo at Luna High*!'

Mr Caldwell smiled. 'Lots of people think that. They think the Moon Colonies are all glitz and shopping and spas but actually the Moon has some of the most spectacular wild open countryside, mountains and manmade lakes. It's a tranquil paradise!' He looked wistfully out at the view.

'Tranquil paradise!' muttered Mercedes. She got up in her seat, turned around to face me, and asked in an accusing tone, 'Did *you* know the Moon was this dusty and clank?'

'I just thought it would be better than Flooded Plains Water Adventure Camp,' I shrugged.

'It better be!' she said darkly, and sat back down in her seat.

Bianca gave me a comforting little *Don't-worry-about-her* face and whispered, 'I think it's going to be amazing!'

The skybus flew lower and lower over the Moon's dusty surface and over the tops of jagged mountains. So close that Felicity was covering her eyes with her hands and mumbling, 'I don't want to die!'

Franka patted her shoulder and said, 'Take deep breaths, Flissy!'

James Defries wasn't helping by talking very loudly

about how many skybuses crash on the Moon's surface every year and telling Louis stuff like, 'Literally no one survived in the 2097 crash over the Tycho Crater.'

Then we saw it: Camp Crater! In its own beautiful dome. Inside there was the zero-gravity floating water funpark, the little mountain ranges for climbing, the Big Showtime Theatre and Float to the Beat dance studios. Under the dome the weather looked beautiful. They'd planted fake trees and bushes everywhere. Everyone went 'Wow!' and started pointing out stuff to each other:

'LOOK AT THE DORMITORY PODS!'

'That's the canteen! The big silver building with the blue lights on top!'

'It looks even better than the brochure!'

'LOOK!' yelled Louis. 'Skycars for kids! What did I tell you, Mercedes?!'

He was right, lined up just inside the main entrance was a row of about thirty of the most beautiful kid-sized skycars. All of them looked better than our skycar at home. Way better. Some were gold, some were crazy hot pinks. 'Just flying my own little skycar is worth coming to the Moon for!' said Louis, leaning back into his squishy chair. And he gave me a little thumbs up, like a thank you.

· ✳·⭐·✳ *

Once inside Camp Crater, Mr Caldwell told us to line up with our dorm buddies. Me and Bianca were with Mercedes, Amia, Franka and Felicity. We stood in our groups with our cases beneath a big floating sign saying *WELCOME TO CAMP CRATER – ACTIVITIES, ACTION AND ADVENTURE!* just staring at everything.

A young woman with a bouncy ponytail called Krissy-Lou led our little group to our dorm pod. She was really enthusiastic. We all walked behind her down the

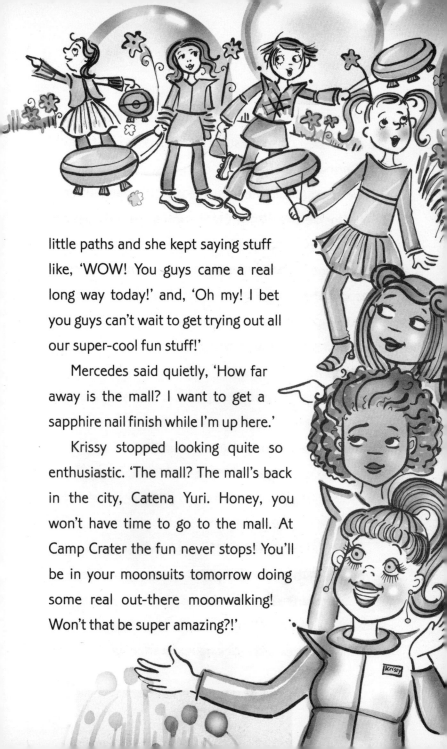

little paths and she kept saying stuff like, 'WOW! You guys came a real long way today!' and, 'Oh my! I bet you guys can't wait to get trying out all our super-cool fun stuff!'

Mercedes said quietly, 'How far away is the mall? I want to get a sapphire nail finish while I'm up here.'

Krissy stopped looking quite so enthusiastic. 'The mall? The mall's back in the city, Catena Yuri. Honey, you won't have time to go to the mall. At Camp Crater the fun never stops! You'll be in your moonsuits tomorrow doing some real out-there moonwalking! Won't that be super amazing?!'

'But is there a skybus to the city?' asked Mercedes as we all climbed up some steps into our dorm pod.

'During your stay you can't leave Camp Crater! That's rule number one here. No kid can leave the camp dome. Inside the Camp Crater dome we have gravity and atmosphere but the Moon is a hostile environment. No one goes out there unless they are protected by transport or a moonsuit. And you have to stay right here in the Camp Crater dome all week unless you go out with one of our super-nice instructors to do moonwalking in your moonsuits.'

She showed us our dorm pod and then she said we'd all be having lunch in the canteen pod at one. 'It's by the main crater lake. And guess what?!' she said, raising her eyebrows like she had the best news ever. 'Today it's caterfilla rainbow noodles and apple bounce! Super yummy! See you there!'

Mercedes didn't even notice the inside of the amazing dorm pod with all its lovely little silver hatches for our stuff. She didn't seem impressed by the cosy sleeping pods all stacked up on top of each other. She just stood there holding her stuff, looking really annoyed.

A MOON BOY LOVES MY FRIEND

'I want the top sleeping pod!' said Bianca, climbing up the ladder and flopping down on the bouncy mattress.

'I'll go on the one next to you!' I said, following her up and checking out my cosy little space. 'Hey, look! It's got mood lighting in here! Look! I made mine show clouds above me.'

'I'm setting mine to stars!' said Bianca.

Felicity said gloomily, 'I don't like heights so I suppose I'll try and be OK in this one down here.'

Mercedes dropped her big moon-shaped pillow down by her feet and said sadly, 'Can't believe we can't go to all the good places in the city. I only came to get my nails done properly.' Then she did a big fed-up sigh and said, 'And I miss Kelvin Cooley *so much*.' She flopped down into a lower sleeping pod, covering her face with her arms and looking all dramatic.

A MOON BOY LOVES MY FRIEND

Felicity said softly, 'It's only a few days, babe. Just keep telling yourself this nightmare Lyla's made us all come on will soon be over. That's what I'm doing!' And she gave me an accusing look.

'It's not a "nightmare", it's FUN!' said Bianca, climbing down the ladder. 'We go actual moonwalking tomorrow! On the actual real Moon! Outside!'

'I suppose we should go to lunch,' said Mercedes, dragging herself up from her sleeping pod. 'Maybe it'll take my mind off missing my Kelvy.'

Bianca gave me one of her little looks. And I mimed holding my heart and fluttering my eyes like a cartoon person in love.

As we both jumped down the steps of the dorm pod Bianca laughed, 'Come on, Lyla! Race you to the canteen.' And we ran on ahead down the beautiful winding paths between rainbow-coloured trees. 'I could live here for ever!' shouted Bianca. 'It's so pretty!'

CHAPTER FIVE

The canteen was full of kids getting their lunch from the dinner bots. The dinner bots were way better than the old ones we have at our school, not rusty at all and not rolling about on old-fashioned wheels getting all covered in bits of mushed-up carrot from the floor. *These* dinner bots had silent jets so they hovered smoothly, like our suitcases.

'Look!' said Bianca, pointing to the piles of food. 'They have blue bananas!'

'Yeah, and check out the desserts!' said Louis, barging about in the queue, his tray already piled high with three blue bananas, two cartons of Luna Lime and a huge pile of rainbow noodles. 'There's apple bounce or

A MOON BOY LOVES MY FRIEND

Moon Shimmer floating ice cream. You can't get that on Earth! Even in Tokyo.'

As I waited in the queue I saw a boy complaining to one of the dinner bots about his lunch. He had the cool Moonite accent and his Moonshades on. He was only our age but he was complaining like an angry grown-up. He was jabbing his finger at the little silver dinner bot saying, 'Listen, Can Face, my noodles are cold! You need to sort this out. And fast.' He jabbed the bot's metal head so hard it wobbled. 'Rainbow noodles are served *hot*, you junkbot! Second day running I've had cold noodles! My dad'll hear about this! Do you know who my dad is? He could get you broken down for recycling tomorrow if he wanted.'

The queue moved forward and I took an apple bounce.

There was only one table with a few spaces left with some kids from another school. We could tell they were Moonites straight away because of the antennae on their heads. They all had that cool Moonite look: great clothes, perfect hair, glossy all over. Just like the Moon girl we had at our school last September. I was a bit nervous because she'd been really mean. Maybe all Moon kids were! I stood still with my tray and my heart beating fast.

'Let's go and meet the natives!' said Mercedes, all confident. So I followed her.

A tall girl turned and smiled at us as we got closer. 'Hi! You guys must be the kids from Earth?' We nodded and I felt a bit shy. A bit shy and a bit scruffy. She went on, 'We're all from the Brightlights Luna Academy in Catena Yuri. I'm Celestia. Join us!'

Mercedes and Amia squeezed into the places next to her. I was about to sit in a space when Celestia said, 'Sorry, honey! That's where Orion's sitting, he's just complaining about his lunch.' She nodded her head

68

towards the boy I'd just seen. 'He does it almost every day! But then he's used to having his own personal ice cream chef at home.' She rolled her eyes, but affectionately, like this Orion was a bit adorable.

I had to share a seat with Bianca.

Celestia waved to Orion as he came back, 'Ori! Look who's joined us today! Earth girls!'

Orion sat down next to me and peered over the top of his Moonshades as he smiled and shook my hand like a grown-up, 'Hi, nice to meet you. I'm Orion Lunablaze. Ori for short.'

'I'm Lyla Hastings and this is my best friend, Bianca.'

'Hi!' said Bianca. Her voice came out a bit squeaky with sudden nerves. She shook his hand.

He held onto her hand for quite a long time and said, 'Hello princess! Are you eleven, like me?'

I groaned but Bianca nodded and went bright red.

Mercedes stood up in her seat to lean over and shake his hand. 'And *I'm* the amazing Mercedes Bonnay, once met never forgotten!'

The Moon kids laughed and Celestia said, 'I'm really loving your hair, Mercedes.'

A MOON BOY LOVES MY FRIEND

Mercedes sat down, patting her green hair, and shrugged. 'Just a little bit of funky Earth-girl style!'

Felicity didn't really join in at all; she was poking at her rainbow noodles and muttering to Franka about them not tasting the same as when her mum does them.

· ✳·✦·✳ *

That afternoon our class had crater climbing. As we all walked over to the indoor crater Mercedes sashayed along in front, saying, 'Oh my total gosh! Those Moonites are the coolest people in the universe. I wanna live on the Moon right now. I am SO moving here when I grow up! These are my kind of people! And you know if I wasn't going out with Kelvin Cooley I would be having such a massive crush on that Ori dude!'

'I know! He's one of those boys who's great looking *and* really nice,' said Amia, giggling.

'I actually think they're a bit full of themselves,' said Felicity.

'Well, I like them!' said Bianca. 'They seem really friendly!'

I didn't know what I thought, so I didn't say anything.

I looked up at the clear dome over our heads and the black starry sky beyond.

The indoor climbing crater wasn't as big as it had looked when we landed. Still, Krissy-Lou said we had to put on helmets and harnesses to climb it. Louis got in massive trouble for running up it straight away without a helmet or a harness and then standing at the top doing a little bow and shouting, 'EARTH BOY CONQUERS CRATER, HARNESS- AND HELMET-FREE!' Mr Caldwell made him come back down and sit on a moon rock next to him for the rest of the session.

Then Felicity said, 'Mr Caldwell, I have vertigo. A terrible, terrible fear of heights. So I can't do it either.' So she sat on another moon rock, while Louis told her the crater was only ten metres high, tops. The rest of us had to shuffle up it in the helmets and harnesses. Even though it was only about ten metres, tops, like Louis said. But you got a good view of the whole camp.

Over on the far side we could see all the kids from the Brightlights Luna Academy doing some low-gravity dancing in the see-through Float to the Beat dance studios.

'They're really good,' sighed Mercedes, watching them do some complicated routine to a distant thumping beat. 'Moonkids can do *everything*.'

When we got back to our dorm pod that evening, there was a little bundle of pale blue moon daisies and a packet of Luna Crystal Mint Bites on the steps outside with an actual handwritten note that said:

To the Earth Princess with the pink hair from ???

Mercedes picked it up. 'That's weird, because I've got *green* hair!'

'It's not for you!' I laughed. 'Bianca has pink hair!'

'What?!' said Bianca. 'Who's it from?'

'Orion?' I said.

'Or maybe *not* Orion,' said Mercedes dismissively. 'Probably just some loon-boon from our school — maybe Louis has a crush on Bianca. I can see that.'

'Louis?! Sending flowers?' I said.

'Yes, he'll have gone a bit funny up here on the Moon,' said Mercedes quickly. 'I bet you it'll be one of our loser boys. I really don't think Bianca is the type to get a Moon boy having a crush on her. No offence, Bianca!'

Bianca studied the little note and whispered to me, 'Well this is embarrassing. What should I do?'

'Give us a Luna Crystal Mint Bite?' I said, giggling and getting ready to go to bed.

Felicity said she had a tummy ache. 'It's those noodles we ate at lunch! I knew they were bad!'

Franka sat next to her and fed her Space Pace tablets like she was a doctor and made her sip a Luna Lime.

When we all turned the lights out Felicity went on complaining, 'Nothing was good today! The skybus broke down. We're not in Catena Yuri, we're basically in a stupid dome in a dusty desert with no shops. That crater climb was a complete waste of time. And we have to talk to those full-of-themselves Moon kids. I'm not sitting with that lot at breakfast . . .'

I was so tired I fell asleep listening to her complaining into the dark.

Next morning we were late. Felicity refused to get out of her sleeping pod for ages, saying she hadn't slept at all. Then Mercedes spent twenty minutes trying to make her hair more 'Moon Camp cool'. She made us wait while she sprayed it and help her decide which clips looked best.

As we walked to the canteen, Felicity said moodily, 'I don't know why you're trying to impress them. Who cares what they think?'

In the canteen Bianca looked around as she got her cereal. 'Looks like we missed them, then,' she said a bit wistfully.

'Who?' I asked.

'The Brightlights Luna Academy lot. Orion and Celestia. They must have gone already.'

Mr Caldwell came round to tell everyone to hurry up as we all had our first moonwalk at nine-thirty and we had to get into our moonsuits and get them safety checked by the instructors before we could go outside the dome. 'We're all meeting at the big sign at the front entrance at nine. Do not be late or we'll miss our time slot! Please read the safety instructions about moonwalking in your dorm pods.'

Mercedes had to change her clips and re-spray her hair again after breakfast. Felicity read the safety instructions out loud to us, but not very well: '"Do not leave the moonwalking area. Follow the instructions . . ."' She stopped reading. 'I can't be bothered. It goes on and on, blah blah, "Don't touch your helmet seal," blah blah . . . *who cares?*' And she sat on her sleeping pod and got another Space Pace tablet out of her flower bag.

There was a knock at our dorm door. It was Louis and James delivering our moonsuits and gravity boots to change into. 'Greetings fellow Moonites!' smiled Louis. 'Your suits for this morning's mission!' And he gave a little salute.

'Did you see the zero-gravity water park yet? It's so awesome! There are kids in there all flying about, splatting into massive water blobs!'

Mercedes turned to look at him. 'We didn't see anything yet because *some* of us are trying to look fabulous!'

'And some of us just want to be back home!' said Felicity, sulkily.

'Uh-oh,' Louis said to James. 'Looks like we've entered a hostile environment of toxic Bad Moodius Oxide!' He did his suffocating thing again, then they both ran off laughing.

Felicity pulled her moonsuit on so slowly.

'Come on,' I said. 'It's after nine already!'

Felicity did her suit up and smeared her face with Mango Moon Protect Plus. At last we set off down the path to the entrance, all clomping along in our gravity boots. Felicity dragged along behind us, complaining, 'I'm so hot. I can hardly walk in these stupid boots!'

'I told you mine would be better!' said Mercedes, doing a few little jumps as she jogged along. 'Like I said, mine have that Lunatex technology.'

'I feel sick,' said Felicity, taking off her helmet.

'Really?' said Franka.

'Yes. It's those horribly bad rainbow noodles I had at lunch yesterday.'

Mr Caldwell said she could go back to the dorm pod until she felt better. We watched her shuffle back down the path.

'There's no way on Earth . . . I mean on *Moon*, I'd miss this!' said Louis, smiling from inside his helmet, watching her plod back. 'This is the best day of my entire life!'

As we got closer to the main entrance Bianca broke into a little jog in her suit and started waving.

'Look! The Brightlights kids are waiting by the entrance in moonsuits too! They must be doing a moonwalk with us!' She sounded really pleased.

We all stood in a big group together while the instructor checked our helmets. Louis was so excited he was doing little jumps up and down saying, 'T-minus three minutes to my first moonwalk!'

Ori smiled at Louis. 'Wow, dude, you never moonwalked? That's crazy! I've been doing them since I was two.' Louis gave him an impressed little nod.

Once we'd all had our suits checked and sealed our helmets, the instructor asked had we all studied the safety instructions in our dorms? Everyone nodded yes. Had we turned on our audio systems so we could hear once we were out? We nodded. He would now lead us outside. He was called Thor. He smiled all the time. His teeth were super shiny and white and he had a Moon-tan. He had on the coolest moonsuit with lots of black and silver squiggles on it. The kids from the Brightlights Luna Academy had really good suits, too. Golden ones with *Brightlights Luna Academy* printed on the back.

'Mercedes was right! Look at us!' laughed James from inside his helmet. 'We're a load of dusty old Earthling losers!'

'Speak for yourself!' said Mercedes, patting her new moonsuit proudly.

As we all shuffled nervously out of the airlock into the big open Moonscape, I felt myself lift and bounce with the low gravity. My tummy felt the same way it does when our skycar at home goes up and down over a stream of flying traffic. I turned to see how Bianca was doing. She looked even more nervous than me, then she fell over, bouncing down in slow low-gravity motion, giggling through her helmet. It was way harder than just rolling about in the low-gravity centre at school. I reached out to help her. Before I could grab her hand, Orion bent down next to her. 'Hey, I'll help you! Let's go bounce about together!'

And off they bounced, leaving me to shuffle and wobble about with James and Louis.

CHAPTER SIX

'OK, let's get bouncing!' said Thor. 'Let's have everyone walk over to the netting on that side and walk back.' But Louis, James and I didn't walk back straight away. Louis started to throw moon rocks through the netting for fun. 'They feel so light! I can chuck one even this big! Watch!' We watched the rock zoom out into the rocky landscape on the other side. I looked up at the blue Earth and hoped Gus wasn't messing about in my room. Louis threw another rock: 'Might get this one into orbit!'

I stared out across the dusty Moon landscape. 'Wow, Catena Yuri! It's so beautiful. How far away do you think it is?' I asked.

'Two miles? Five?' said James.

Louis threw another stone up and over the fence. 'Yeah, five miles max!'

'You're not supposed to throw moon rocks out here,' said James.

'Says who?' said Louis, pinging a little moon pebble up over his head and watching it land somewhere right behind the Camp Crater dome.

'Says the safety instructions we all *said* we read.' James smiled.

'I'll just throw little pebbles.' Louis pinged another one so that it zoomed right over the camp dome. 'Look at that go!'

'Bianca's having fun,' said James, turning round.

I looked back at the big group of kids shuffling about with the instructor, Thor. Thor had put on some kind of funky music and was making everyone do a silly dance, getting everyone to jump around and wave their arms in the air. Bianca was laughing with Orion. Orion was doing some backflips. I could see Mercedes trying to copy him in her pink and purple moonsuit.

Thor waved over to us three. 'Come on, guys! Join

in! We're moon dancing! This is crazy fun, guys! You don't wanna miss this!'

'Wanna bet,' said James quietly, mimicking Thor's Moon Colony accent. 'Come on, we better go back and join in. We don't want to look like a bunch of sad loser Earthlings.'

By the time we'd shuffled back over Thor had turned off the music and was saying, 'YOU GUYS WERE AMAZING! GIVE YOURSELVES A BIG CAMP CRATER CHEER!'

Everyone from our school just went, 'Yeah!' and 'Woo!' But all the kids from the Brightlights Luna Academy seemed to know a whole Camp Crater chant off by heart. It had lots of weird hand claps and air punches and went:

A MOON BOY LOVES MY FRIEND

Camp Crater is the best!
Better than the rest!
Gimme one!
Gimme two!
Touch my moon shoe!
Gimme three!
Gimme four!
Eat a Moon Camp s'more!

Mercedes was singing the chant as we walked back to our dorm pods to change out of our moonsuits. She had memorised the actions already.

Felicity sat up in her pod when we all came back to the dorm. 'What happened out there on the moonwalk?'

'It was amazing!' I said. 'You have to go next time. It's so strange!'

'The moon kids had the best suits!' said Franka. 'We looked really scruffy!'

'*I* didn't,' said Mercedes, flopping back onto her sleeping pod. And she sang a bit more of the chant, doing some of the actions with her hands above her head as she lay there. 'Those Moon kids are really cool.'

'Yeah,' said Bianca, laughing, 'and they've been doing moonwalking all their lives so they're all really good at it and don't fall over like I did.'

'Oh yes! Big news, Felicity!' squealed Franka. 'Bianca fell over and that Ori boy helped her!'

'He was just being nice,' said Bianca, brushing out her hair.

A MOON BOY LOVES MY FRIEND

'So it must have been him who sent her the flowers!' shrieked Franka.

'We don't know that for sure,' said Bianca, biting her lip. 'And if it was him, he's just being friendly.'

'No, take it from me. I know about this stuff!' said Mercedes. 'He's totally in love with you! Sending you mints and daisies! Hanging out with you all through the moonwalk! The guy's crazy about you! I know it's kind of weird with him being so cool. But it's true love!'

Bianca wrinkled her nose and shook her head. 'No one is in love with me. I don't want them to be.'

Felicity lay back on her sleeping pod and carried on looking at moon ponies on her interface and eating some more Space Pace tablets. 'Anyway, who wants a Moonite boyfriend,' she said in a sullen voice. 'Who wants a Moonite *anything*. I just want to go home!'

That evening Bianca sat next to Ori and Celestia in the canteen. But there were no more spaces on that table. 'Sorry, Lyla,' shrugged Ori. 'There's a space over there with your crew!' So I carried my tray of moon rice and strawberry flower cakes across the canteen to sit with James and Louis. Louis was talking with his mouth full, swigging great gulps from his two cartons of Luna Lime. 'The thing that's going to be awesome is when we get to drive those kid-sized skycars! D'you think we get to take them outside on the Moon or just round the inside of the camp dome?'

'Dunno,' said James. 'Be good if we could have a massive sky race out on the Moon like in a movie.'

'Yeah! To Catena Yuri and back!'

I stopped listening and looked over at Bianca. She was putting on her fake Moonite accent to make Ori laugh. He was saying, 'We don't sound like that!' and flicking bits of flower cake at her for fun.

Bianca was flicking some back and going, 'Stop it, Ori! It's going in my hair!'

A MOON BOY LOVES MY FRIEND

I was glad Orion and Celestia and all the Brightlights Luna Academy kids had to tidy their dorm pods that evening. Bianca and I could be together. But Bianca only wanted to talk about them. 'They come every year, Ori told me. They always have a residential trip here. That's how they know all the songs.'

'And I bet they don't have to do about five million bake sales to get here.'

'No, they don't. Well, they only have to come five miles from Catena Yuri. It's local for them.'

We walked on through the little fake flower-lined winding lanes between other schools' dorm pods. Ahead we could see Ori and Celestia sitting outside their tidied dorm pod, chatting. Celestia had on one of those tops that shows how fast your heart is beating with little pulsating daisy flowers all over it. As we walked towards them I sighed, 'Can we not talk to them for too long? I know they're nice but . . .'

Before I could finish, Bianca overtook me, patting her pink hair into place. 'Hi, Ori! Did you tidy your dorm already?' She was almost running now.

I followed her.

Celestia smiled her beautiful smile. 'Hi, guys! We were just talking about you. *Again!*'

'Oh?' I said.

'Well Ori was just telling me about when Bianca was falling over in moonwalking and how he had to help. And how funny she was doing the moon dancing!'

Bianca went bright red and giggled, 'I know! I was hopeless. But we haven't *all* been doing it since we were two!' She gave Ori a playful pat on his arm.

Suddenly I felt a bit left out, so I tried to get myself back in by saying, 'I like your top, Celestia, we can't get those on Earth. But we see them on all the shows like *Lucy Loo at Luna High.*'

Celestia laughed and said, 'Oh my! Do you guys still get that old show? My cousin was actually in it!'

'Wow,' I said, but actually I've only ever seen it once, and I didn't like it much. And I remember Gus making sick noises all through the episode we watched because there was a load of kissing. Though I didn't say this to Celestia.

'She's in proper movies now,' said Celestia, like it was no big deal.

No one spoke for a bit; Ori and Bianca just stood smiling at each other and I was about to tell everyone about Louis throwing the moon rocks, just for something to say, when Celestia said, 'You guys wanna go into Catena Yuri while you're up here?'

'Oh, we're not allowed out of the camp all week,' I said. 'That Krissy-Lou told us when we arrived. We have to stay in the Camp Crater dome.'

'Yeah,' nodded Bianca, 'Mr Caldwell won't let us go either, we'd need permission from our parents and stuff.'

Celestia raised one eyebrow like we were crazy. 'But it's only a few miles away. We usually go in the free time on Thursday after the drama session.'

'Are you lot allowed to leave camp?' I asked.

'Not *technically*,' shrugged Ori.

'But we go anyway. We creep out every year. No one notices,' laughed Celestia. 'We just hang out at the big mall for a bit. You should come. I *have* to go because I have a date with my boyfriend.'

'Do you walk there?' said Bianca, looking uncertain. 'In moonsuits?'

'No way!' laughed Celestia, tossing back her swishy hair. 'Waaay too dusty! We all have skycars. You must have seen them, parked at the front entrance.'

'We thought they belonged to the camp,' I said.

'You really have your *own* skycars?' said Bianca, excited. 'That's so cool!'

'Yep. Kids can drive skycars at aged nine on the Moon. That's how we came to camp, we all drove here,' said Ori, casually.

'Wow!' said Bianca, impressed. 'You Moon kids are really grown up!'

Ori smiled. 'It's just normal here, the skycars are really easy to use and safe. I got my new one just last February when I turned eleven. When we go you can have a lift in mine,' he said, nodding at Bianca.

Bianca went red again and giggled.

'Well,' I said firmly. 'She— *we* can't go. None of us can. Like I said, we have to stay inside the dome all week.'

A silly little plinky plonky tune came through the speakers, followed by Thor's super-excited voice telling us all that free time was over and we should return to our dorms and 'Get some sleep – because remember kids . . . ACTIVITIES, ACTION AND ADVENTURE NEVER STOP AT CAMP CRATER!'

'Come on, Bianca. We have to go,' I said.

As we walked away, Ori said, 'Even if you two don't want to go, tell that girl Mercedes and her friends about going to Catena. But not everyone! Just them. We'll sneak out about two, after the drama session on Thursday. We can meet by the fake bushes and hide near the big sign.'

I turned back and shook my head to say *no*.

'Go on! It's nothing! We go every year!' He was yelling now. 'Bianca? You'll go, right?'

'Say NO!' I hissed at Bianca. 'It's stupid!'

But Bianca smiled over her shoulder. 'Maybe! I'll ask the others!'

We started to walk a little faster back to our dorm pod. 'You can't be serious!' I hissed. 'Don't tell the others, Bianca! It's so stupid. We'll get in massive trouble!'

'They do it every year! It's fun!' she said, doing a little skip over a fake daisy.

I just carried on walking and looked down at my feet. Bianca spun round to face me, grabbing my right hand in both of hers. 'Come on, Lyla! Don't be like this! You got us up to Moon Camp, you should be into this. It's a real adventure! I wonder what Celestia's boyfriend is like?'

I carried on stomping along, just saying nothing and still looking down.

'They've been driving since they were nine!' went on Bianca. 'It's only a few miles! It's the same as us flyking from your house to the Trading Hub. Ori will give us a lift. I bet he's good at driving.'

'*Ori, Ori, Ori,*' I muttered crossly as we walked into our dorm pod.

When we got inside, we couldn't talk about Ori any more because Felicity was sitting on her sleeping pod crying loudly and blowing her nose, with Franka and Mercedes hugging her.

Amia was running about trying to get a signal on Felicity's chatcom. She was waving it around above her head. 'Don't worry, Flissy! If I climb up onto Bianca's top bunk we might get a signal.' Amia scaled the ladders up to Bianca's top bunk, and carried on trying to get Felicity's chatcom to work.

'What's happened?' asked Bianca, sitting on the sleeping pod next to Felicity and Mercedes.

'She's *really* homesick,' said Mercedes, very seriously.

'She needs to talk to her mum,' added Franka. 'It's an emergency.'

Felicity sobbed even louder and wailed, 'I CAN'T STAY HERE! I HATE, HATE, HATE THE MOON!'

'Yeah! We have a signal!' shouted Amia. 'Shall I call your mum?'

Soon the hologram of Felicity's mum's head hovered in our dorm. The reception was really bad, though, so half the time Felicity's mum looked like she had half a head or pixel eyes.

'Hi, baby!' Felicity's mum waved. 'How's my big, brave girl?'

'MUM!' yelled Felicity, in between massive sobs. 'COME AND COLLECT ME! YOU HAVE TO COLLECT ME! I MISS YOU SO MUCH!'

But Felicity's mum said it was only four more sleeps and then Flissy would be back in her own bed with Terry Teddy and Blanky Boo and that she was looking up at the Moon every night and blowing Flissy a thousand kisses.

Eventually Felicity calmed down and wiped the watery snot off her nose and agreed she would be a big, brave girl. She ended the call and sighed.

Mercedes put her arms round her and said, 'It's tough missing someone special, like me missing Kelvin Cooley. It's really tough! Us two just have to be brave.'

'You should call him!' said Felicity, brightening up. 'Call him! And we can all see how hot he is!'

'Nah,' said Mercedes, wrinkling her nose. 'It's OK. He'll be busy.'

Felicity looked down at her crumpled half-eaten packet of Space Pace tablets and sighed, 'I just wish Camp Crater wasn't so . . . far away from home and so . . . boring.'

'It's not boring!' I said. 'The canteen's great and the moonwalk was brilliant! Louis threw a rock out there and it went for about a mile! Plus it's drama in the Big Showtime Theatre on Thursday! And blaster archery tomorrow!'

Everyone ignored this.

Bianca smiled a little secret smile and looked sideways at Felicity and said, 'Well . . .' And I just knew what she was going to say before she said it. 'We *could* all go to the mall in Catena Yuri. That would be *real* fun!'

I gave her a big-eyed, *have-you-lost-your-mind* stare.

Which she didn't notice because Felicity had grasped her hand and was saying, 'Oh my total gosh, that would make me SO happy!'

'How do we get there?' said Mercedes. 'Is there a skybus?'

Then Bianca said, with a toss of her hair and a raised eyebrow, 'I have a friend who can give us a lift.'

Mercedes grasped her knee. 'Your boyfriend Ori!'

'He's not my *boyfriend*, silly! Just a friend. But he *does* have a skycar – all those Moon kids do! They're the skycars by the entrance. And every year they sneak off in one of the free time sessions to go to the mall!'

'Yes! I'm finally gonna get my sapphire-finish nails!' said Mercedes, standing up and twirling round.

'And I can get Mummy a really nice present!' said Felicity. 'I'm not homesick any more! Thank you, Bianca!'

'We can see all the buildings and Moonite girls in their crazy outfits like in *Lucy Loo at Luna High*!' said Amia.

'And we're NOT ALLOWED TO LEAVE THE CAMP!' I added, crossly. I stood there like a teacher with my arms folded across my chest. 'This trip is because of me! I can't be creeping off to the mall! What if we all get hurt by a crashing meteor or something? Everyone will blame me.'

'Crashing meteor! *As if*,' said Mercedes. 'Come on, Lyla, it's not *your* trip. We all did the bake sales. I bet you want to go as much as the rest of us. We'll be like an hour, tops!' And then they went on blabbing about going to Catena and shopping till they drop.

· ✳·⭐·✳ ·

They whispered about it all night. About how much money they'd need and how much a crystal bikini costs and how handsome Ori was. I kept interrupting with, 'But we're not allowed to leave the camp!'

It was useless, I was just a squeaky little whisper

in the dark that no one heard as they were all busy discussing if Bianca got married to Ori later would she actually move up here to the Moon. And part of me did really want to go to the mall and see the city and the 'Optimum Living Experience'.

And maybe I was just a bit fed-up Bianca had a boyfriend now, who I didn't even like. What was the point of me risking getting into massive trouble for an afternoon trailing about Catena Yuri if I'd be with Bianca giggling and Ori telling her he never knew Earth girls could be so amazing?

I lay there thinking these things over and over. I think I fell asleep as Mercedes was saying she and Kelvin Cooley would have a house in Catena Yuri with a purple low-gravity splash pool and a stable for moon ponies.

Then I had a horrible dream about crashing off the Moon into black space in a very rusty old skycar being driven really badly by my brother Gus and Louis.

CHAPTER SEVEN

I felt a bit better at breakfast because it was brilliant at Camp Crater. They had a buffet with tonnes of stuff you can only get up on the Moon, and not just the blue bananas. They had about fifteen different cereals — even Peach Bubbles and Fruit Jewels.

Louis was sticking some of the little ruby raspberry things on his nose.

'Idiot,' muttered Mercedes, eating her muffin.

'What? Don't you like my designer nose? I thought you'd love it!' he laughed. 'It's blaster archery this morning! Cannot wait!'

I ate my Peach Bubbles sitting next to Bianca. I whispered, 'Are you really going to go to Catena Yuri?'

'What? Who's going to Catena Yuri?' asked Louis, eating the little red jewels off his nose. 'Is there a trip going? I thought it was blaster archery and free time this afternoon.'

'It is,' said Mercedes, giving Bianca a conspiratorial look over her cereal.

'Yeah,' said Bianca, looking back at Mercedes with just a hint of a smile. 'No one's going to Catena, we're not allowed.'

Later, Bianca and I walked slowly towards the Blaster Archery Zone. 'So if we did go to Catena Yuri,' I said, 'would you be going round with Ori all the time?'

'So you *are* going to come!' She smiled. 'I knew you would!'

'I didn't say that.' I thought about the view of Catena from the skybus when we arrived. The Armstrong Tower, the massive stadium, everything bright and new and amazing. 'But what if we get caught going out of camp?'

'We won't!' said Bianca. 'Ori says they never get caught. And so what if we do? It's worth it! It's a real Moon adventure! Not like this blaster archery — hardly an adventure, is it?'

I looked over at everyone lining up and putting on the ear defenders that Thor was giving out. Thor was handing out red blasters to the people at the front of the lines and giving out instructions. 'These Moon blasters are totally safe, and they are modified so they have only enough power to hit the targets. That said, guys, do *not* point them at each other!'

I saw Louis looking just a little disappointed as he handled the blaster. It looked like a toy – nothing like the massive silver ones you see on the news.

Thor clapped his hands to get everyone's attention again, 'So, if you all take a look down the firing range, you can see our fun Camp Crater targets. Krissy-Lou is a bit of an artist and you can see her super line-up of EVIL ALIENS!' At the end of the firing range there was a row of quite badly painted big aliens, they looked only a bit better than something Gus might make. They were silly, painted in pink and green with googly eyes. Bianca and I walked towards everyone and got in line. The kids at the front had already started to fire their blasters. *Pop. Pop.*

Thor said we'd be put in teams and score points.

Bianca gave me a look and said under her breath, 'So, Lyla, is this a Moon adventure? Or is this just another boring PE lesson?'

I didn't answer, I just put my ear defenders on and waited for my turn.

Louis and James were having a really funny conversation at lunch about how James hadn't hit a single alien and how the blasters looked like they came out of Christmas crackers. I wanted us to sit with them but Bianca waved and shouted, 'Hey Ori!' across the canteen. 'Can we join you?' So we sat with them. Then Mercedes and Amia joined us with Franka and Felicity, squeezing in so our table was almost too crowded to put all the trays on.

'Hey, Ori!' said Mercedes, helping herself to one of his chips, and looking around before whispering. 'We going after drama tomorrow?'

'Sure,' he smiled, taking a swig of his Luna Lime. 'After drama. By the big sign and the main airlock entrance. Hiding by the fake bushes. You lot all coming?'

Everyone except me nodded excitedly.

Felicity said, 'You bet!'

Ori nodded and said, 'Great,' and chomped on through his chips.

'Where do you guys want to go first when we get there?' asked Celestia.

'I want my nails done with a sapphire finish!' said Mercedes. 'So I need to go to the main mall.'

'OK,' said Celestia, 'that's easy. Anywhere else?'

Everyone just looked excited and shrugged their shoulders. 'Well, we'll all meet after drama. But just you lot. Don't tell anyone else: remember we can't fit your whole class into two skycars!' And everyone laughed like this was hilarious.

'No we won't,' said Mercedes, her eyes all bright and excited. 'Just us lot. The coolest Earth babes!'

I woke up really early that Thursday morning.

And all morning I didn't say much, even in our session in the zero-gravity water park which was really funny. Everyone was floating about, crashing into the giant floating blobs of water, screaming and laughing, but all I could do was worry about the plan to leave camp.

After lunch Bianca whispered to me as she put her leftover food in the degraders: 'Drama, then . . . *you know what*! You'll come, yeah?' She was all excited.

'Maybe,' I said. 'Maybe I'll come. Are you going to be hanging out with Ori all the time?'

She shrugged. 'I guess we'll all be going round in a big group together. It'll be fun!'

· ✳·⭐.✳ *

The Big Showtime Theatre was on the far side of Camp Crater, right near the edge of the dome. It was way better than anything we have at school, with proper lights and seats.

Bianca looked around the auditorium. 'Oh look! The Brightlights lot are up there. I can see Orion!' she said, sounding relieved. She waved up at them.

Ori waved back. 'COME AND SIT UP HERE WITH US!' he yelled.

'Do we have to?' I said. 'We're much closer to the stage here.'

Anyway, Thor and Krissy-Lou made everyone sit together at the front near the stage. 'Come on, guys!

All to the front seats. Drama at Camp Crater is interactive, you're not here just to watch! You're here to become CAMP CRATER SHOWTIME THEATRE STARS!' Everyone whooped and clapped and the Brightlights Luna Academy burst into another loud chant, standing up, with all the hand movements. Mercedes joined in. 'OK! OK!' smiled Thor, 'Great energy, guys! Now usually we all have a go at being a hologram pop star, but it seems the equipment has been damaged recently by a high velocity rock.' He looked mildly concerned. 'I know none of you have been throwing rocks out on your moonwalks, I know all of you understand how fast a rock can travel here up on the Moon with the low gravity outside the dome.' I saw Louis slide down in his seat a little. Thor went on, 'It was probably caused by a small meteor. Anyway, it's left us with no hologram equipment, but . . .' Thor paused to look all dramatic. 'We can go back to the ancient art of . . . *mime*.'

About half our class groaned and Mr Caldwell gave us a massive, 'Ssh!'

Thor asked for volunteers. A few of the keen Brightlights lot ran up, but only Burak from our class joined them. And he only did it to get laughs by pulling extra silly faces as Thor made them all pretend to be eating a bowl of imaginary noodles. I heard James whisper to Louis, 'How long do we have to sit here? This is boring.'

'Burak's not boring,' laughed Louis. 'Did you see him stick his tongue out just then?'

'I could watch Burak sticking his tongue out for laughs back at school,' muttered James. 'I did not come three-hundred-and-ninety thousand miles for *this*!'

'Nor did I!' whispered Bianca, looking sideways at me. 'Is *this* an adventure, Lyla? Is *this* what we did about a zillion bake sales for? A stupid drama lesson?'

I didn't answer. I looked at the kids onstage now pretending to put on imaginary moonsuits and do imaginary moonwalking. And I realised James and Bianca were right, this *was* boring. Had I really come three-hundred-and-ninety thousand miles for this and a bit of blaster archery with plastic blasters? I turned to Bianca and whispered, 'OK. I'll go to Catena Yuri with you lot. But we've got to be sensible. And we're not coming back late.'

Mr Caldwell whispered, 'Enough chat, Lyla! Show some respect to the children onstage!'

Bianca grasped my hand in the dark and whispered, 'Yes! It wouldn't be the same without you. Catena Yuri! That's what we made all those cakes for, Lyla!'

CHAPTER EIGHT

Bianca and I made our way nonchalantly towards the main entrance, pretending we were just on a little walk. Mercedes said we'd all look less suspicious if we didn't go as a big group, so she and Amia were going to count to a hundred in the dorm pod and then start out behind us, followed by Felicity and Franka.

'Look!' said Bianca, as we got close to the main entrance. 'I can see Ori's silver jacket in the fake bushes. He's there.'

Soon we were all huddled together in the fake bushes.

Felicity giggled nervously, adding some shimmer shine to her lips. She whispered, 'I want to look super-cool when I'm there!'

'OK,' said Ori, poking his head up out of the bushes. 'All clear. Run into the airlock and we'll all get into the skycars!'

'Isn't this fun!' giggled Bianca as she ran, hunched down, towards Ori's skycar and got into the seat next to his.

Mercedes jumped into one of the backseats behind Ori, patting his hair as she jumped in saying, 'Nice little skycar!' and Amia got in next to her. Franka and Felicity had jumped into Celestia's. I really wanted to go with Bianca.

'Come on, Little Sprouty!' whispered Ori, out of his skycar window. 'Get into Celestia's before the security bots come around again!'

Little Sprouty.

Suddenly I felt like walking back into the camp and just sitting about with Louis and James for the rest of the afternoon. But Celestia was tooting her silly horn at me. I clambered into her little pink skycar and sat next to Felicity in the back.

Celestia put on loud music when we were flying and chatted to Franka, 'We can't go very high, cos we're kids.

That's Moon law.' Ahead we could see Orion's silver skycar doing some crazy swerves and loop the loops. Celestia smiled, 'He's such a show off!'

'He better not crash!' I said firmly. 'Look how close to the crater he's going!'

'He's fine! His dad's some kind of intergalactic pilot.'

I could imagine Bianca and that lot having lots of laughs and chatting and shrieking as Orion zoomed his skycar about. Meanwhile I was stuck next to Felicity who spent the whole journey telling Celestia how long she'd had her soft toys for. She had to shout above the loud music from the back seat: 'I'VE HAD BLANKY BOO SINCE I WAS ONE!'

I looked out of the little windows at the dusty Moonscape. I could see solar power stations in the distance: huge, revolving circular plates winking in the light. I stared at Earth and imagined Gus pottering about after school with his Moon Wars sets and playing with Sparks. Celestia was talking about the best place to get a sapphire nail finish in the mall but I had stopped listening and just gazed up at the sky and a line of big sky lorries far above us, bringing all kinds of deliveries into the city.

We flew low over the top of a crater and then suddenly the huge dome that encased the whole of the city of Catena Yuri was in front of us. Like a huge half

bubble full of the sparkling city. It looked just how it does in the movies, only bigger and better. 'WOW!' I said, leaning forward in my seat and clutching onto the back of Franka's.

'Well it *is* called the "Big Sparkle",' said Celestia proudly. 'I forget, living here all my life, just how amazing this place is.'

'So much traffic!' I said, looking around. All kinds of skycars, skybuses and rockets zoomed in and out of the dome. Above us were those massive flying cruise rockets that bring tourists from all over the galaxy.

The one making its steady way above us had *MARS LINERS* written on it in huge letters. Celestia confidently turned her little skycar to one of the airlock portals which said 'Residents' Entrance Only'. And then we were through the dome and into the most amazing city I'd ever seen. I pressed my nose up against the skycar window, just like my little brother, Gus, when he's in ours at home and he's spotting all the different makes of vehicle. The buildings were so tall, Celestia had to weave her little car between them. 'Everything is so new and shiny!' I said. 'Look, Felicity! Look at the blue banana trees in the lobby of that massive silver hotel!'

But Felicity had her nose pressed to the window on her side. 'Oh my total gosh!' she squealed. 'I swear I just saw the actual Luna High School from the TV show.'

'Probably,' said Celestia, slowing down as she approached the famous mall. 'It was made round here.'

Ori had already landed his skycar on the mall launch pad and we could see the others walking about and pointing at everything. Mercedes was filming on her chatcom and Bianca was excitedly waving back at her. Ori had his arm round Bianca's shoulder and was giving Mercedes a thumbs up.

'We made it!' shouted Mercedes, jumping up and down as we got out to join them. For a few minutes we all just stood looking in every direction, up at the little fake white clouds, the crazy tall buildings and the strange smell of the Catena air.

Bianca sniffed, 'Why does it smell so *good* in here?'

'Our atmosphere is treated to smell like this.' Celestia smiled. 'I don't even notice it any more. Does the Earth smell bad?'

'Only when my little brother farts!' I laughed.

'Yeah! Or Louis in maths!' added Bianca.

Orion and Celestia smiled but they didn't laugh; they looked at us like we were just a little bit beneath them.

'Right!' said Celestia, like a mum. 'Shall we check out this famous mall and get those nails done?'

I'm not really a mall person. I'm not usually much of a shopping person. But it was all so sparkly and different, even *I* felt excited as Celestia strode ahead of us like a tour guide. Ori was just behind, chatting to Bianca, whispering funny little comments to make her laugh.

He stopped walking. 'Actually guys, me and Bianca might go and get a Glowshake at the Sparkle Shake Shack. Shall we all meet back at the launch pad at three-fifteen?'

'Can I come with you two?' I asked.

'Lyla, duh!' said Mercedes. 'It's a *date*! Leave them alone.'

Bianca didn't hear me anyway. She walked away with Ori, laughing and tossing her hair about.

The rest of us followed Celestia. 'Check out the Bubbleators!' she shouted to us, pointing above her head. We looked up at the high, high crystal dome ceilings and noticed people rising to all the different levels, floating in their own personal bubbles. 'Too bad the nail bar is on this floor!' she laughed.

'What's up on the higher levels?' I asked.

'Everything!' she said. 'The food hall. Galaxy sweets. Luna Toys. You could buy a kid's skycar from Luna Auto if you had enough money. In Catena Yuri you can get everything you can imagine. Nothing's teleported in. Nothing's virtual. It's all right here!' she finished proudly, walking towards the nail bar. Mercedes was almost breaking into a jog to get there faster.

When we got closer we saw a boy about our age waving at Celestia. 'Hi baby! I missed you so much!' he said.

Celestia ran up to him and gave him this massive hug and a kiss. Not just a little kiss but like a grown-up movie kiss! Then, still holding his hand, she smiled at us. 'Guys! Meet someone very special! Felix Tranquility X! My first boyfriend. Isn't he beautiful!'

A MOON BOY LOVES MY FRIEND

We nodded politely looking at his very smooth skin and super-shiny hair. Of course Mercedes said what we were all thinking: 'Err. He's just a cyborg kid! That's not a *real* boyfriend!'

Celestia narrowed her eyes. 'How can you say that, Mercedes?! You Earthlings are so primitive and prejudiced! Of course he's real! And my daddy bought him for me!' Then she stroked Felix's cheek and said softly, 'You *are* real, aren't you, baby?'

'Yes, Celestia, my angel. Our love is real and for ever!'

Mercedes looked down at her feet. 'Sorry I said that. Um. Nice to meet you Felix Tranquility X.'

'OK, let's forget all about it and get those nails done!' said Celestia brightly, slightly dragging her electronic boyfriend into the shop.

Felicity held back. 'You know what, thinking about it, my mum won't want me to have my nails done. She says I'm not old enough.'

'*Really!*' said Mercedes, looking incredulous. 'The sapphire finish only lasts two weeks. What's her problem?'

Felicity looked offended. 'She doesn't have a *problem*. She just thinks I'm too young.'

Mercedes shrugged her shoulders. 'Suit yourself.'

I looked up at all the amazing levels of crazy Moon stores and the people floating up in the Bubbleators. 'Actually,' I said, 'I don't want my nails done either. I'll go off and explore and meet you lot back at the launch pad.'

Felicity sighed. 'I guess I should come with you, then, Lyla.' She said this like it was a bit of a chore. 'S'pose it's better than just waiting here.'

'Or you could just watch while I get mine done?' said Franka.

Felicity looked at her best friend, and then back at me. She looked at me like I was a disappointment. 'No, it's OK. I'll go with . . . *humph* . . . Lyla.'

Felicity is not someone I've ever spent any time alone with. We're not exactly friends. But we're not enemies. We just hang about in the same group. She's been really mean to me in the past. But we're kind of OK now. Still, going round the Moon mall with her for an hour did feel like I was about to go round with some distant relation.

Like a cousin you only see at Christmas, or more like an auntie, as Felicity is a bit like a mum. I would have rather gone by myself. We started to walk away from the nail bar.

'Shall we get a Bubbleator?' I said. 'I'd like to see Luna Toys, there might be something small I could get for my little brother.'

'Those Bubbleators don't exactly look safe,' said Felicity, gazing up. 'I'm not sure my mum would want me going in one.'

'Well, she's not here, is she?' I smiled. 'Come on! We're only in Catena Yuri for a little bit. Let's check out the Moon toys!'

Felicity dragged behind reluctantly.

To get into a Bubbleator you had to stand on a little metal circle on the floor. Then a huge clear bubble formed around you and a nice calm robotty voice said, 'Greetings! Where may we take you today?'

'Toys?' I said, a bit nervously. The bubble began to float up into the high mall with me inside. Below I saw Felicity getting into hers and beginning to float up. I waved cheerfully, as she was looking nervous.

My bubble floated up to the fifth level then floated towards the entrance of Luna Toys. As soon as the bubble touched down by the store entrance it popped. Just like a small bubble popping when it hits the ground.

I watched as Felicity's bubble landed and popped. 'That was weird!' she said, but she was smiling. 'It wasn't too scary, was it?'

'It was fun. Can't wait to go back down!' I said. 'Come on! Let's see what these flashy Moon kids play with.'

CHAPTER NINE

The toy store was huge. They were letting kids take their shoes off at the main entrance and try out jet socks for free. So the store was full of buzzing sounds as little kids zoomed up and down and all around the store, their brightly coloured jet socks puffing out blue vapour trails.

Felicity and I walked about the store. We agreed we were a bit too big for jet socks. I guess we're almost too big for toys too, but I told myself it was OK as I was actually looking for a present for my six-year-old brother. We looked at the mini cyborg fashion dolls doing a little catwalk show up and down a table. We stared for ages at the floating replica Moon that hovered and rotated in the air. It had all the Luna cities on it, lighting up on the shady side. They had Moon Wars battle rockets but not the tiny ones Gus plays with at home – bigger ones that a small toddler could actually fly around in.

Felicity couldn't stop looking at the robot pets section. 'Lyla! Look at the little green monkey! Look at the elephant! I could take that to school in my bag, he's so small!' The strange little animals were wandering around a fake mountain landscape. Then Felicity saw something else and darted towards a display at the back of the store. 'Lyla! LOOK! Micro pugs!' She stood by a display of a little fake park and put her hands up to her cheeks in total amazement as she watched tiny pug dogs romping about. They truly were the cutest teeny-weeny robotic pugs. Fluffy, in pastel shades, with sparkling collars around their necks and adorable big eyes. But only as tall as the top of your thumb. 'How do they work?' Felicity asked the cyborg assistant.

'Solar-powered. Just leave them in sunshine for about thirty minutes and they're back up and ready to play,' she smiled. 'You can train them to talk *and* sing!'

'That's better than my old electronic cat, Sparks,' I said. 'He can't speak.'

'How much?' asked Felicity, starting to open her little flower-shaped bag.

The assistant told us and I backed away in shock, saying, 'Whoah! You're kidding! For something so *small*? It'll probably get lost by next week! Sucked up by a vacuum bot!'

'The charms on their little collars are *real* diamonds,' said the cyborg lady in a haughty voice.

'So gorgeous!' whispered Felicity, lingering by the little pugs and looking wistful.

'Come on, Felicity. I should have a look for something cheaper for Gus. I'm going back to the front where the small Moon Wars stuff is.'

The only thing I could afford was a really small tube of that stuff called Invisabalm. There was probably only enough in the tiny tube to turn one of Gus' feet invisible, but I knew he'd love it. The instructions said the effects lasted for up to six hours, so I thought Gus could have a fun day at school with an invisible foot.

Felicity walked over to me quite quickly, almost like she was in a rush. 'You finished?' she asked.

'Yes, I got him this.'

But Felicity didn't really look, only said quickly, 'How about we get out of the mall now and see some other sights?'

'Oh. I wanted to look at the food hall. Don't you want to see all their crazy Moon cereal and fruit?'

Felicity walked on. I had to almost break into a run to keep up. She stood on the Bubbleator circle to go back down.

'What about looking at the Moon crystal fashion place?' I yelled. 'They have real crystal shoes. Like Cinderella!'

'Come on, Lyla!' she said from inside her bubble. 'There's more to Catena Yuri than shopping. I'm going back to the ground floor.' Her voice was a little muffled by the bubble.

When we had floated back down and stepped out of our popped bubbles, I said, 'Shall we go and see the others? See how their nails are going?' But Felicity was making her way to one of the huge exits that led out of the mall. 'No. We'll meet them on the launch pad at three-fifteen. Come on!'

'Why are you in a hurry?' I said as we came out of the mall onto one of the long straight avenues of Catena Yuri.

'I'm not,' she said, slowing her pace. 'I just get . . . a bit . . .' She paused to think. 'I'm actually mall-phobic. I have a fear of malls.'

'Since when?' I frowned.

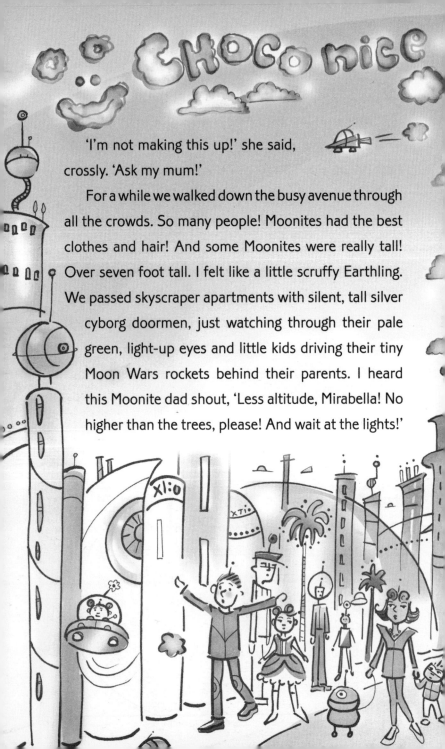

'I'm not making this up!' she said,
crossly. 'Ask my mum!'

For a while we walked down the busy avenue through
all the crowds. So many people! Moonites had the best
clothes and hair! And some Moonites were really tall!
Over seven foot tall. I felt like a little scruffy Earthling.
We passed skyscraper apartments with silent, tall silver
cyborg doormen, just watching through their pale
green, light-up eyes and little kids driving their tiny
Moon Wars rockets behind their parents. I heard
this Moonite dad shout, 'Less altitude, Mirabella! No
higher than the trees, please! And wait at the lights!'

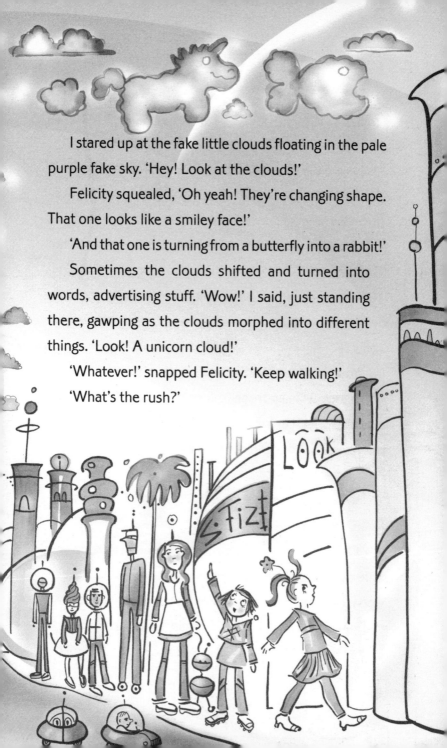

I stared up at the fake little clouds floating in the pale purple fake sky. 'Hey! Look at the clouds!'

Felicity squealed, 'Oh yeah! They're changing shape. That one looks like a smiley face!'

'And that one is turning from a butterfly into a rabbit!'

Sometimes the clouds shifted and turned into words, advertising stuff. 'Wow!' I said, just standing there, gawping as the clouds morphed into different things. 'Look! A unicorn cloud!'

'Whatever!' snapped Felicity. 'Keep walking!'

'What's the rush?'

'Obviously, I need to get far away from the mall to get over my phobia!' she said. And we walked on.

'Look, a Kitten-Me Salon! We don't have *those* in the Trading Hub,' I said. 'Let's go in. We could really surprise everyone if we came back with those adorable fluffy ears and some real whiskers! Better than sapphire nails.'

'Lyla, if my mum won't allow me to have my nails done, why would she want me coming home half kitten?!'

'You won't be "half kitten"! It says, "Your beautiful kitten look will last three to four days." Look, they have a special offer: cat iris eyes, fluffy ears *and* whiskers. You can have shimmer-pink *or* gold fur.'

'Come on,' Felicity said, yanking me a bit too hard.

'Where are we going? We don't want to get lost,' I said, a bit puffed.

'OK, that's far enough,' she said. 'Let's just sit in this little park here. And wait till it's time to go back.' Felicity walked over to sit on a crystal bench under some blue and pink Luna trees. The coloured leaves rustled in the fake breeze.

A MOON BOY LOVES MY FRIEND

'What's the time?' I asked.

'Two forty-five. We'll just sit here while I get over my, um . . . mall-phobia. Then we'll go back to the launch pad.'

'You do look a bit pale and scared,' I said.

'I am,' said Felicity. 'I'm having a really bad attack of mall-phobia. I should probably take a Space Pace tablet to calm me down.' She put her hand into her little flower bag and took out a Space Pace. But as she did, some small, furry things jumped out and scuttled under the bench.

'OH NO!' she screamed. 'WHERE DID THEY GO?'

'What?'

Felicity began scrabbling about under the bench frantically.

'What are you looking for? What was it?' I asked, crouching down to look with her.

And then I spotted them, sitting by the roots of a tree.

Soft, silky fur, teeny black faces and the cutest eyes. 'Micro pugs!' I said softly, picking them up and handing them back to Felicity. 'You bought two *micro pugs*? Are you *crazy!* They're so expensive! How much pocket money do you get?!'

'None of your business!' she snapped, plopping the teeny little robotic dogs back into her flower bag and snapping it shut. 'Let's start walking back to the launch pad.'

We walked back up the avenue. 'We didn't see any sights, really, did we?' I said.

'We saw all this.' Felicity gestured around her at the Moonites walking about and the buildings. As we came to the mall entrance, she said, 'Actually, how about we walk around the mall and find the launch pad that way. Let's have a little explore.'

A MOON BOY LOVES MY FRIEND

'We might get lost,' I said. 'It's much quicker to go the way we came, straight through the mall.'

Felicity looked at me like I was stupid. 'And what about my mall-phobia? Have you forgotten that?'

'No. Sorry. We'll go your way.'

We walked a few paces on past the mall entrance, following the curve of the building. We could see the launch pad ahead. Then something very strange happened. I couldn't move. I felt stuck.

As though my feet were glued to the pavement. Felicity turned to me. She was also stuck. I looked back over my shoulder. A woman in some sort of official-looking uniform was coming towards us. In one hand she held a gun-like gadget that she pointed at our stuck feet.

'Got you!' she said in her Moon Colony drawl. 'You two better come with me to the head office.'

I stared wide-eyed at Felicity and whispered, 'What does she want? Maybe we needed some kind of documents to be out here? What do you think we did wrong?!' I felt my heart beating about a thousand times a minute.

When she came close to us she pressed a button on her glue-gun thing and we could move our feet. 'Don't you two even think about running off. The securobots saw you. Let's go, girls!' Then I heard her mutter to herself, '*Earthlings*, it's always Earthlings!' under her breath. 'That whole planet's a bunch of backwards thieving scumballs!'

· ✳·⭐·✳ *

The woman in the official-looking uniform sat behind a smooth desk. She had taken us to a small circular room somewhere on the ground floor of the mall. She asked us both to show her what we had in our bags. I showed her the Invisabalm, but she wasn't interested. Felicity was being extra-slow opening her flower bag. 'Come on, come on! We haven't got all day,' said the woman. 'I think you might have put something in there without paying.'

That's when Felicity stopped opening her bag and started crying. Tears rolled down her cheeks. 'I need to call my mum!' she wailed.

The woman sighed. 'Let's have a look at what's in the bag, first.'

Felicity placed her half-eaten packet of Space Pace tablets onto the desk and then the micro pugs.

'You didn't pay for these, did you?' said the woman.

Felicity stammered, 'I wasn't stealing! It was a mistake!'

'Does it *look* like a mistake?' the woman said, one eyebrow raised, and showed us a very clear hologram of Felicity playing with the micro pugs about half an hour ago in the store. The hologram showed Felicity looking about, making sure no one was looking, and then very quickly and carefully hiding them in her flower bag. Felicity just stared at her feet.

I glanced at the time. It was already three-fifteen!

'Can I call our friends?' I said. 'We need to meet them now!'

The woman rolled her eyes and sighed, 'All right.'

I got out my chatcom and called Bianca. Bianca looked panicked. 'Where are you?'

'We're in a bit of . . . trouble,' I said, not really knowing what to say. 'Can you wait for us, I don't know how long we're going to be.'

Ori's face came over the chatcom. He looked really angry. 'No way, Sprouty! If we don't go right now, we'll never get back in time. I don't know what stupid Earthling trouble you're in. And I don't care. You can make your own way back!' And he ended the call.

Felicity started to cry again, only louder, shuddering and gulping. 'IT WAS A MISTAKE! . . . *bwaah* . . . CALL MY MUM! . . . *bwaah* . . . She'll sort this out. She'll tell you I'm really nice and good!'

'Let's do that now,' sighed the woman, looking just a bit sorry for Felicity.

Felicity's mum cried almost as much as Felicity, but between her sobs she said that darling little Felicity was usually the goodest child you could possibly meet in the whole universe and she could only imagine the change in atmospheric pressure on the Moon had affected Felicity's brain and she would be more than happy to pay the full price for the micro pugs herself. She looked a lot less happy when she heard how much they actually cost.

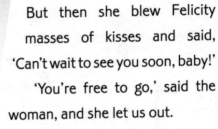

But then she blew Felicity masses of kisses and said, 'Can't wait to see you soon, baby!'

'You're free to go,' said the woman, and she let us out.

'RUN!' I said to Felicity. 'IF WE RUN STRAIGHT THROUGH THE MALL WE CAN GET THERE IN TIME!'

As we ran Felicity shouted stuff at me between breaths: 'My mum's right! It was the Moon's atmosphere that made me do it! And if it wasn't for you, Lyla, none of this would have even happened!'

'You were the one who stole two micro pugs worth gazillions,' I puffed as I ran.

'Because of the atmosphere!' she wheezed back, starting to believe her mum's theory. 'I wouldn't have ended up stealing anything if we'd gone to Flooded Plains Camp back on Earth. It's obviously *your* fault for doing all your stupid bake sales and getting us here!'

CHAPTER TEN

'WE'RE TOO LATE! THEY'VE GONE WITHOUT US!' wailed Felicity as we skidded onto the launch pad. 'They left us here to . . . DIE!'

'We're not going to *die*,' I said.

'But we *are* stuck here,' said a voice behind us . . . Bianca! Still on the launch pad, sitting on the railings, shielding her eyes against the afternoon sunlight. 'Celestia took the others. I asked Orion to wait but he wouldn't! They went about twenty minutes ago.' She got down off the railings and walked across to us. 'He was so horrible. I'd rather have a cyborg boyfriend like Celestia's. Actually I'd rather not have one at all!' She laughed.

'Thanks for waiting,' I said.

She smiled.

'But . . . now what?' I said. 'We can't walk back. No moonsuits!'

Felicity sat down on the floor and started to cry. 'I can't even do moonwalking! I didn't do the session! THIS IS THE WORST RESIDENTIAL TRIP EVER! We're stuck here for ever! We're going to DIE! Here! And my mum will die of a broken heart!'

I crouched down next to her. 'We'll call Mr Caldwell.'

'No!' shouted Felicity. 'I can't be in any more trouble today. You two can find a way to get back to camp! Though how are you going to do that? You can't bake sale your way out of this stupid mess!' she added angrily, and wiped watery snot from her nose.

'So, I'll call Mr Caldwell,' I said, trying to stay calm.

'NO! He'll yell at us! I can't be stressed out any more! I'LL CALL MY MUM!' Felicity began looking in her flower bag for her chatcom. 'She can send a Luna taxi up to collect me right NOW!'

'That'll cost tonnes!' I said.

'Wait!' said Bianca. 'Look over there, Orion's coming back!' A little skycar was heading back to the launch pad.

A MOON BOY LOVES MY FRIEND

'That's not Orion's,' I said, as the skycar came closer. 'It's pink. Celestia is coming back to get us!'

But it wasn't Celestia. It was *Louis*! Louis landing Celestia's skycar, his cheeky face peering out at us, doing a double thumbs up in the driving seat, sitting next to Mercedes.

Louis yelled out of the skycar, 'That was amazing! Did you see me land it?'

Mercedes called out of her side, 'No offence, Bianca, but your boyfriend is a jerk!' while admiring her new blue sapphire nails.

'For the ninetieth time,' laughed Bianca, getting into the backseat, 'he's NOT my boyfriend!'

'Let's go, Lyla! Flissy! Come on!' shouted Mercedes. 'If we go right now we'll be back before they notice!' We jumped in. 'Louis, swap places!' said Mercedes. 'My turn to drive!'

'Am I the best at this or what?' said Mercedes as she swerved the little pink skycar over the craters. 'Probably all that stuff I do in my Persojet at home. I'm a natural!'

'Did you ask Celestia if you could borrow this?' I asked.

'Yeah. Kind of,' said Mercedes.

'Kind of not really.' Louis smiled, turning his head to look over his seat at me. 'Celestia will never know.'

'You stole her car?' I said, thinking we Earthling kids really were a 'bunch of backwards thieving scumballs'.

Louis explained. 'When Mercedes got back and said those Moon kids had just dumped you at the mall, I said we should "borrow" a skycar and come and get you. This is a legitimate rescue mission!' He looked out at the curved white horizon of the Moon and the Earth beyond.

A MOON BOY LOVES MY FRIEND

'She'll go crazy if she finds out,' I said.

'Lyla, I had no choice,' said Louis. 'It was either make moon rock bracelets with Krissy-Lou all afternoon or a rescue mission in a skycar over challenging Moon terrain. No contest!' Then he laughed and grabbed the controls in front of Mercedes. 'Come on, do some stunts before we get there!'

Back in Camp Crater, Mercedes parked the little pink skycar. Then we hid in the bushes like before and one by one sneaked our way back into camp. Mercedes went first, then Louis, Bianca and lastly me and Felicity. Just as I got through the main entrance Felicity shouted, 'Lyla! Wait! I dropped the micro pugs when Louis did those stupid stunts. Help! Help me look!'

'But we're late!'

'*Please!* Mummy spent a fortune on them.'

The micro pugs were just on the seat inside, running around in tiny circles. 'You didn't even *need* me,' I said as we began walking back through the entrance, straight into . . . Mr Caldwell.

He looked as angry as I'd ever seen him.

'RULE NUMBER ONE! DO NOT LEAVE THE CAMP!'

'We didn't!' stammered Felicity. 'We were just walking near the main entrance in our free time.'

'That's not what I heard just now from a security guard from the Catena Yuri Mall! She's just called me. Thought I might like to know what two Earthling girls from my class had been doing this afternoon!'

A MOON BOY LOVES MY FRIEND

Then he said we were so late back we had to go straight to the canteen to eat. He marched us in silence through the winding paths of fake flowers. Before we went in to eat he made us stand in front of him by a fake palm tree and said we had caused a huge amount of disruption and anxiety and we had let down the whole school. 'What do you think these Moonites think of you? They must have a very poor impression of Earth children now! Leaving camp. Stealing! You have not only let down the school, but your whole planet!'

Felicity looked down and bit her lip. Then Mr Caldwell said that there would be no last moonwalk tomorrow morning but instead the whole class and all of the Brightlights Luna Academy kids would have to go to a meeting in the Big Showtime Theatre to find out just how we ended up in Catena Yuri and who else was involved.

As we walked away from Mr Caldwell, Felicity tossed her pigtails and smirked to herself. 'Like I care Mr Baldwell! I got micro pugs!'

Everyone was already eating their apricot clouds and blue bananas when we walked into the canteen.

There were hardly any noodles left.

I walked through the noisy tables with my tray. Bianca waved to me, 'Did Caldwell catch you?!' she whispered.

'Yes.'

'You never told me why you and Felicity were so late,' she said.

'Felicity stole micro pugs and we got caught.'

'No way!'

'We had to be interrogated for ages,' I said glumly.

'Did she give them back?'

'No. Her mum's paid for them.' I rolled my eyes. 'You know what her mum's like.'

We looked over to where Felicity was showing off her new micro pugs to Franka and Amia. They were all going, 'Aaah, super cute! What are they called?'

Mercedes was chewing her apricot cloud. She raised one eyebrow and rested her chin in her hand. 'Yeah, they're super-cute but everyone's saying you . . . *stole* them.' She gave Felicity a hard look.

Felicity looked all wide-eyed and innocent. 'That's what it looked like, but it was because my brain was affected by the different pressure up here on the Moon. It was an innocent mistake! I don't know what happened! I have zero memory about it!'

Franka patted her hand and said, 'Poor you, Flissy!'

'Anyway, they're mine now and Mummy paid for them,' said Felicity, smiling and stroking the tiny robot dogs with two fingers. 'I'm going to call them Pinky and Pebble.'

Bianca and I watched the micro pugs scamper between the plates and bowls. We rolled our eyes at each other – a silent 'Yeah right!'

· ✳·⭐·✳ *

Later, Bianca and I walked back towards the dorm pods. Celestia and Orion were sitting outside their dorm, watching us approach. When we got closer, Orion stood up and sort of blocked our way.

'Hi, Ori,' said Bianca quietly. He didn't answer for a bit. He looked angry.

Celestia looked up at us. She was wearing some new Moonshades she'd bought in the mall, and she peered over the top of them. 'We need to talk.'

'About what?' I said.

'About you not saying anything about us two leaving the camp in the meeting tomorrow!' said Orion. 'Us lot have been sneaking out from camp every year, no problem, but you stupid thieving Earthlings had to mess everything up! I *can't* be in trouble. If you tell on us tomorrow, you'll really get it!' He came really close to my face and said, 'Remember, Sprouty, my dad's a top intergalactic pilot!'

'So what?' I said.

'*So*, he's really important!'

'What's that got to do with anything?'

For a second Orion looked like he'd run out of things to say.

Then Celestia added darkly, 'I think Orion's just saying his dad could . . . make things difficult for you if you get Orion into trouble.'

I wrinkled my nose. 'Yeah, right! I'll be three-hundred-and-ninety thousand miles away from here in two days. Come on, Bianca, let's go!' And I linked my arm through Bianca's as we walked away.

A MOON BOY LOVES MY FRIEND

Felicity was training her micro pugs to do tricks in the dorm until really late. When we finally all got into our sleeping pods, Mercedes said, 'That mall was amazing! I really don't care how much trouble I get into tomorrow. I got my sapphire finish nails!' And she wafted her hands about, looking at them shimmering in the light.

I lay in the dark, listening to everyone as they fell asleep. Then I whispered to Bianca, 'Do you think we will get in massive trouble tomorrow?'

'Don't know,' she whispered back.

'Are you sad about Orion not being your boyf—your friend any more?'

'No!'

'Bianca, do you think it would have been better if we'd gone to Flooded Plains Water Adventure Camp?' I whispered into the dark.

I could almost hear her thinking it through. Then she whispered, 'No, I'd rather be in massive trouble at Moon Camp than avoiding giant rats in Norfolk!'

CHAPTER ELEVEN

After breakfast everyone had to go to the Big Showtime Theatre. Burak wasn't pleased. As we all wandered in, he muttered, 'I'm missing my last moonwalk just cos some idiots had to get their nails done!'

Mr Caldwell made me and Felicity stand on the stage next to him while he spoke to the other kids. 'Yesterday, these two girls decide to leave camp and go to – can you believe it? – Catena Yuri! You were all told you are NOT allowed to leave the camp grounds. That is rule number ONE here!'

Thor and Krissy-Lou were standing with their arms folded, nodding and looking stern. Thor stepped forward. He frowned at the crowd of kids, scanning the worried faces staring back at him. 'We'd like to know who else went to Catena Yuri yesterday?'

There was an awkward shuffling about in the crowd, but no hands went up.

Except for Bianca. 'I went, too,' she said. 'Sorry.'

Mr Caldwell got her to stand next to me and we linked our pinky fingers to give each other support. 'Anyone else from Lime Grove Edu Hub?' said Mr Caldwell, his arms crossed.

'Me and Amia and Franka,' said Mercedes, standing up. All three joined us up onstage. They walked up slowly, heads down. Mr Caldwell asked us why would we do such a silly and dangerous thing and Mercedes blurted out, 'Well, obviously, Mr C, most of us wanted to get a sapphire nail finish!' She waved her fingers under his nose.

Mr Caldwell looked up to the ceiling and shook his head, 'A sapphire nail finish!'

Thor spoke: 'Well, these Earthling girls didn't *walk* to Catena! And the only children here with skycars are from the Brightlights Luna Academy.' He looked accusingly in the direction of the Brightlights lot. No one spoke. No one moved.

Thor turned to us. 'Maybe you three would like to tell us how you got to Catena.'

On the front row next to Celestia sat Orion, his eyes were mean little slits as he stared right at us, shaking his head very slowly and mouthing at Bianca, 'Don't . . . tell!'

Bianca just looked down at her feet.

A MOON BOY LOVES MY FRIEND

Then Louis put up his hand and said, 'Can't say who took 'em there. But I got them back.' He joined us onstage.

Celestia looked at Orion, her eyes wide and puzzled. She mouthed the word, '*How?*'

Orion stared at me. I stared right back. I thought I could stare them into admitting. But instead Celestia made her hands do that Moon swearword at me, and this time it didn't look funny like when Louis showed James on the skybus, it looked mean. Her sapphire nails flickered as she made the sign.

Krissy-Lou saw it. 'I think we need to see your fingernails.'

Slowly Celestia showed her hands.

Her beautiful blue nails twinkled with a perfect Catena Mall sapphire finish.

'You better come and join your friends up here,' said Krissy. By the time Celestia got up onstage, hot tears were falling down her cheeks. 'This isn't fair! It wasn't just me that took them. Orion took them too!'

'No I never!' he shouted back. 'She's lying! I don't have my nails done, do I? I never went!'

A MOON BOY LOVES MY FRIEND

It took nearly an hour for us to explain the whole thing to Mr Caldwell and Krissy-Lou. Everybody tried to explain it all at once.

'Well, I just wanted sapphire nails!' said Mercedes.

'I was only trying to help! It was an emergency!' shouted Louis. 'Earthling kids stick together! It's a fact!'

'Calm down, Louis!' said Mr Caldwell.

'You stole my car!' spat Celestia.

'*You* left Lyla and the other two in a hostile Moon environment!'

'I left them at the mall, stupid!' said Celestia. 'And what about Orion?! He was mostly responsible.'

Then Orion started to cry a little bit and said, 'Bianca *made* me go! She bullied me all week! She's a pink-haired bully! Like her little friend, Sprouty! My dad's right, he always says Earth kids are rough and mean!'

'My name's *Lyla*, not Sprouty, and you know we didn't bully you!' I said, folding my arms.

Then Mr Caldwell said, 'That's quite enough!' and

said we would all be missing the free time session that afternoon to stay in our dorm pods, start packing, and 'Have a long think about being sensible and responsible campers.'

We didn't.

We talked about Catena Yuri, and sapphire nails, and how we couldn't get everything back into our cases, and how even Louis MacAvoy would be a better boyfriend than Orion Lunablaze.

· ✳·✰·✳ ·

Early the next morning Mr Cuddon arrived in his big old skybus with *Sneddon's Skybuses – To the Moon and Beyond!* on the side. He said it was all fixed and 'Good to go!'

We all lined up with our floating cases. Mr Sneddon began loading them onto the skybus. As we shuffled forward to get onto the bus, Bianca and I looked over at the line of kids' skycars and the Brightlights Luna Academy lot putting their bags into them and preparing to go. Suddenly Bianca turned her head away. 'Uh-oh, look who's coming over!'

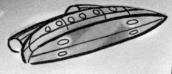

Orion was walking towards us, his head bowed. He came up to Bianca, looking kind of small and sorry.

'I will miss you, Bianca,' he said. 'And I am sorry. My dad goes crazy about me being in trouble.' He gave her another packet of Luna Crystal Mint Bites.

'Um, thanks,' said Bianca, looking embarrassed.

'Come on at the back of the line!' shouted Mr Caldwell. 'We need to get back in time!'

'Well, I have to go now,' said Bianca as we stepped up onto the skybus. 'Bye, Ori.'

We watched Orion walk back to his little skycar as our big skybus took off and began to make its way up into the black starry sky.

'THERE! WHAT DID I SAY?! I TOLD YOU HE WAS TOTALLY IN LOVE WITH YOU, BIANCA!' shouted Mercedes over the top of her seat.

Bianca went bright red
and put her head down.
'This has all been so
cringey!' She winced.
'Now I wish we HAD
gone to the boring
Flooded Plains
Adventure place!'

'Really?' I said.

She looked out at the big blue Earth getting closer
as we flew home. 'No. Not really. Moon Camp was a real
adventure.'

I smiled. 'With added cringe.'

· ✳ ⭐ . ✳ ·

The skybus didn't break down on the way home. We
watched the Moon grow smaller and smaller as we flew
back to Earth. The cities of the Moon faded out of sight,
just clusters of twinkling lights.

After about an hour Mercedes said to Amia,
'You know, a trip like that, it changes you for ever. I
feel I'm a whole new person and that's why I'm . . .'

She paused to be all dramatic, 'I'm finished with Kelvin. It's over!'

'No!' said Amia. 'He'll be devastated!'

'Or relieved!' shouted Louis, over his seat. Before Mercedes could yell anything back, he stood up in his seat and said, 'Guys! Time for a song!'

And we all sang 'We're a Mile in the Air But We Don't Care!' so many times by the time we landed Felicity's micro pugs could sing it as well in their squeaky little voices.

Felicity was the first person off the skybus, pushing ahead of everyone down the aisle. 'MUMMY! THE MOON WAS AMAZING!' She jumped down the steps and gave her mum a massive hug.

'And did you try everything, my big brave girl?' said her mum.

'Yes!' nodded Felicity. '*Almost* everything! And I was really good at loads of the activities!'

I rolled my eyes at Bianca.

Bianca whispered, 'Complaining was one of the activities, right?'

· ✳·⭐.✳ *

When I got home, Gus was really happy with the Invisibalm present. 'I deserve it!' he said. 'Because I never went in your room. Not once. Not even my big toe went in!'

'Good,' I said.

'Was Moon Camp fun? Was it better than the Flooded Plains Big Rat place?'

'Way better. And we all went there because of me!'

Gus rolled his eyes, 'Blah blah, "because of me."
Come on, let's make our noses invisible. Or our ears?'

'Both,' I said. 'We'll do both, then we'll go and
show Dad.'

The
End

HOPE JONES
SAVES THE WORLD

JOSH LACEY
ILLUSTRATED BY BEATRIZ CASTRO

My name is Hope Jones. I am ten years old. I am going to save the world.

Hope Jones' New Year's resolution is to give up plastic, and she's inspiring others to do the same with her website hopejonessavestheworld.com. When she realises her local supermarket seems to stock more unnecessary plastic than food, she makes it her mission to do something about it. She may be just one ten-year-old with a homemade banner, but with enough determination, maybe Hope Jones really can save the world.

'A lively and heartening read'
Guardian

9781783449279